To Kai

Wolf Spirit

The Story of Moon Beam

Love
2010   March.

By
Beverly Lein

INKWATER
PRESS

PORTLAND • OREGON
INKWATERPRESS.COM

www.inkwaterpress.com

ISBN-13 978-1-59299-466-3
ISBN-10 1-59299-466-0

Publisher: Inkwater Press

Printed in the U.S.A.
All paper is acid free and meets all ANSI standards for archival quality paper.

1 3 5 7 9 10 8 6 4 2

I would like to dedicate this book to friends and families in Sunny Valley and surrounding communities where I grew up.

To Dianne Smyth my editor who prods, pokes, for a better story sentence because as she puts it, it's inside you girl, let's hear it.

For her belief in me and my stories.

Last but not least to my grandchildren Brittany, Morgan, Sydnee, Rachel, and Ashley my inspirations.

There is nothing more important than creating a story and the love of reading.

There is nothing in the world as precious and unique as you five.

I love you God bless you all

Table of Contents

CHAPTER 1

Abandoned

It was winter, in the late 1840s ...

Ten-year-old Rachel walked over to the bed and whispered, "Mommy are you awake. I'm cold. The fire's almost out." There was no response from the figure lying on the bed.

The sickness that had killed her father, Morgan, two weeks earlier took Rachel's mother that night. The heartbroken little girl crawled up on the bed, lifted the heavy moose hide cover, and slid into bed beside her mother. "Oh Mommy don't be dead, please don't be dead, please Mommy ... I'm scared ... don't leave me." She wrapped her tiny arms around her mother's neck. Sobbing and frightened the little girl lay beside her mother's body holding her tight. But as the cabin grew colder so did her mother's body.

Some time later the frightened child crawled from the relative warmth of the covers. The floor was cold on her feet and she looked around for her moccasins in the semi-darkness of the cabin. She found her clothes first and pulled them on over the long underwear she wore during the winter months. Finally, thoroughly chilled, she found her moccasins under her bed and quickly slipped her feet into them. Rachel sighed deeply and looked at the fireplace where only a few coals still smouldered, knowing that she would have to get the fire going before it went out completely as it would be hard to start a new one. There were a lot of wooden matches up in the cupboard but it was ever so much easier to stoke the fire from the coals. She went to the wood box where three pieces of wood were left from the night before. Rachel picked them up along with the small pieces of bark that lay in the bottom of the box, and took them to the hearth where she laid them aside. Crouching down close to the floor she blew on the coals as she had seen her mother, Brittany, do so many times before. As the coals came to life she carefully laid the small pieces of bark on them till they burned freely, then put the last of the logs on the fire with great care to make sure she didn't suffocate the flames. As the wood started to burn she realized that it wouldn't be long before the fire went out again.

After wrapping herself in her coat, she put on her outside moccasins, and then pulled her beautiful fur-lined mitts over her trembling hands. She started to sob again as she remembered her mother's laughter when she was cutting out the pattern to make the mitts. Britanny had lovingly sewed the soft pieces of beaver hide and squirrel fur together with strips of sinew from the moose that Daddy had shot. Her father had been a trapper and was meticulous in his ways. Nothing was ever wasted, neither the meat nor the hides of the animals. He always made something useful out of the remains, be it clothing, footwear, bedding, tools and utensils, or weapons. Her parents had been resourceful people who took great pleasure in creating things out of next to nothing.

With tears running down her cheeks, Rachel opened the door and the cold winter morning rushed in, taking her breath away as she stepped outside into the bitter cold. The crisp snow crunched under her feet as she slowly headed for the woodpile.

Daddy cut wood all summer long when he wasn't out trapping or hunting. How exciting it had been to watch the trees crash to the ground. Daddy would hook his horse, a huge black stallion he had broken himself, to the big trees and skid them home to the cabin. In the late summer and fall, many days were spent cutting trees for winter firewood. When all the trees were neatly stacked near the cabin, he spent hours chopping them into blocks while Rachel and Britanny piled them up against the cabin.

Rachel picked up as much wood as she could carry and walked slowly back to the cabin. She liked the quietness of the cold morning, in spite of the tears freezing to her cheeks. Entering the cabin she put the wood into the box and went back for another armful. She avoided looking at the body of her mother lying on the bed. After dumping her second armful she decided to bring as much in as she could possibly carry, hoping she wouldn't have to go out in the dark later in the evening. She knew she'd be scared to go out alone without her mother waiting in the cabin. Fear suddenly consumed her. The northern Alberta winters were always so long and cold. This was only February and there were no other humans around for miles and miles.

Daddy liked being out in the wilderness, away from other people. It wasn't that he didn't like people, but too many of them just made a crowd. He had discovered this beautiful valley with the river running through it and moved his family there years ago. Rachel could not remember living anywhere else. The river near their cabin was called the Mighty Peace and he had named their kingdom Sunny Valley. Daddy built them a cabin snuggled into the bank of the river, high enough up that it wouldn't flood in the spring. Sometimes the river did flood with the ice jams and a few times it came close to the cabin. Mommy worried and paced up and down, but Daddy would just laugh and say, "You worry too much Brittany."

Their cabin was about twelve feet by twenty-four feet. Daddy had dug deep into the bank with a shovel, almost making a cave. Then he shored up the insides with logs, so that only an edge of the roof was visible from the top. The chimney came up through the ground above and was barely visible. The whole area was heavily treed and had an abundance of bushes. The door was made of heavy wood and was so well constructed and levered that even Rachel could open it, but just barely. Daddy always barred it from the inside at night. A battering ram couldn't knock that door down. Two small windows on each side of the door with shutters that opened inward were the only source of natural light in the cabin. In the summer they left the door and the windows open during the day, unless the bugs were bad.

At the back of the cabin, behind a huge cupboard, was another door with no handle. Even with the cupboard pulled out, it looked like part of the wall. Inside was a root cellar where the dried salted meat was hung. The pantry stayed cold in the summer and in the winter the meat stayed frozen. It was so well insulated that animals could not smell the food. The bags that Mommy made from animal hides were filled with dried berries: saskatoons, blueberries, blackberries, cranberries, raspberries, strawberries, and chokecherries, which hung from hooks on the wall. Other things like horseradish, cabbage, beets, radishes, wild onions, corn, carrots, peas, beans, potatoes, and squash were stored in there too.

Daddy had made a garden on the flats near the river, which was about a quarter-mile from the cabin. Even if someone found the garden they would have a hard time finding the little cabin. Daddy didn't worry much about animals but people were a different story. He had known some pretty rough characters in his time. The lush black dirt along with the hot sun and the occasional rain ensured a thriving garden that produced most of the food they needed to survive. Every other day in the summer the little family packed a lunch and went down to the garden for three or four hours.

In the very back of this root cellar was another recessed cavity, a secret cavern. Its opening was small and was completely hidden by huge shelves. By moving aside the hides and furs on the shelves they could crawl into it and then stand up, even Daddy. The secret room went deep into the bank and had vents at the surface that were hidden from view, as were the root cellars.

It was a good hiding place, a safe place for Rachel and her mother when Daddy was away. Once inside, they could slide the hides back in place and be completely invisible. Daddy worried about them a lot, especially since the visit from that disgusting man who had wanted to hurt Mommy. And sometimes the Indians came. They were always stealthy and they came too close for comfort. Mommy didn't trust them. Daddy said the Indians were good people and that there was no reason to fear them. But Rachel and Mommy were always scared of them because they looked so fierce. Besides, they had read about Indians and some of the stories about them were terrifying. Mommy had brought a quite a few books when they moved from civilization to the wilderness, as she was determined to educate Rachel about the world. As far as Mommy and Rachel were concerned you couldn't be too careful when it came to Indians, despite what Daddy thought about them.

All these thoughts were running through her mind as she packed one more load of wood into the cabin and shut the door. Hunching down by the fire she wrapped her small arms around her knees and rocked back and forth sobbing. She was alone.

Rachel had heard her parents talking about a camp that was about sixty miles away from their cabin. Daddy told them there was an Indian village there. The thought crossed her mind that the Indians might help her, but she was too afraid to take that chance. Mommy had always told her to stay away from the Indians and to make sure she was completely out of sight if they came around. In Rachel's ten years she had seen only a few Indians and one Whiteman.

One time two Indians got badly hurt by a big grizzly and Daddy had come and got Mommy and Rachel to help. There was no shortage of food for bears in Sunny Valley, so the grizzlies didn't bother about people at all. Unless, of course, they thought their cubs were in danger. But the Indians were very wary of this particular grizzly — he wasn't an old bear but he was what they called a "rogue" bear. None of them seemed to know what had turned this bear into a killer. He attacked at will, not for food or out of fear, but just for the sake of killing. The rogue was so bold that he frequently strolled into unsuspecting Indian villages to grab a young child or a dog. If the dogs attacked him they didn't survive and several Indian braves had been swatted to the ground by his great claws. This grizzly killed its own kind as well. The female grizzlies, when trying to protect their cubs from him usually died, along with their babies.

The Indians had repeatedly warned Daddy to watch out for the grizzly, and told him that if he ever got near enough he must kill the beast. They told him that he would be able to identify this bear because, for some strange and possibly supernatural reason, he had white tips on the points of his ears.

Despite her fear of the Indians, Mommy had stitched and bandaged the wounds of the two injured men, and after she was done Daddy helped them get back to their village. The Indians liked Daddy and often brought him fruit and vegetables from their gardens. After the mauling he traded with them on a regular basis. Rachel and her mother began to think that maybe the Indians were all right after all.

But the Whiteman was a different story. He had terrified Mommy and Rachel. He was a dirty repulsive man with broken front teeth. One day, when the two of them were packing water up from the river he appeared out of nowhere, riding towards them on his horse. His movements seemed slow and relaxed, but his eyes were shifting everywhere, taking everything in as he came closer. Rachel and her mother were startled and frightened because he had appeared so suddenly. Because of the strong wind and the rush of the river, neither of them had heard him ride up.

Mommy hesitated, and then cautiously greeted the man as he swung himself off the back of his horse. But in that moment, both Rachel and her mother sensed that this man was bad. He paused and leered at Britanny. Rachel had no idea what this meant, but it didn't look good. She started to back away as the man walked towards her mother. Britanny stood there defiant and challenging, trying not to show her fear.

Suddenly, without any warning, the man grabbed her. "How about a little kiss ..." he said ... lunging for her. Rachel froze as her mother, in one swift and powerful motion kneed the man hard in between his legs. He fell back swearing and gasping for air. Rachel knew it was time to get help and she ran as fast as her legs could carry her.

What she saw next was just a blur, as Daddy came flying out of the bush right in front of her. With seven or eight long strides he was on the evil man, smashing him into the ground. Rachel stopped in her tracks, speechless and unable to move. When her father was done with him he helped the man back on his horse. She saw that the man was missing a few more teeth and had a bloody face and a crooked nose. One of his arms dangled at an unusual angle and his shoulder seemed to be hanging really low. He was moaning and groaning. Rachel heard Daddy tell him that if he were ever seen around this neck of the woods again, he would put a bullet right through his head. There was no doubt that the whimpering man believed him. And so did Rachel.

She thought back on this event for some time. Rachel didn't know about other Whiteman but if they were anything like this one, it's no wonder her father had brought them to Sunny Valley.

The nearest settlement was a town they called Peace River. It was ninety miles away, and Rachel didn't know if it was upriver or downriver. Daddy went there every spring to sell his hides and again in the fall to get supplies for the winter. Rachel and

Britanny always stayed home. Daddy was usually gone for about two weeks, and would suddenly arrive home loaded with wonderful things. He'd have seeds for Brittany's garden, and bags of flour, sugar, salt, coffee, matches, bullets, and many other essential supplies.

The biggest treat for Rachel was a bag of her very own filled with candies, tiny toys, and other delights. Sometimes, he'd bring her a doll and doll clothes if he had been able to find them. He always brought material for Britanny so that she could make beautiful dresses for the two of them. Not that they had anywhere to go, but they did like to dress up on Sundays.

Daddy always said that when Rachel turned twelve he was going to take her and Mommy back to civilization. Only two more years! Rachel had been anxiously waiting for this birthday. It wasn't that she didn't want to stay with her many animal friends, but it sure would be nice to have a real friend. She used to imagine what it would be like to have a friend, someone her own age. Over time, she'd had plenty of imaginary friends but she always yearned for a one, someone she could share things with, one she could talk to. Of course, there were times that she really didn't want to leave Sunny Valley. For one thing, she couldn't possibly leave her animals behind. They would have to come too.

Rachel sat in front of the fire thinking of all the things her father had talked about. But what good would any of it do now? She was all alone. Rachel turned and looked at her mother lying lifeless on the bed. How she could possibly bury her all by herself.

When Daddy died her mother was still there with her. Between them they had wrapped Daddy in moose hides, tied the hides tight around him, and then, they gradually pulled and tugged until they got his body outside. Mommy dug a deep hole in the snow and they gently rolled Daddy into the bed of snow. After that Mommy and Rachel piled wood from the woodpile on top of his body. Mommy told her that they would dig a grave and give him a proper burial in the spring.

Rachael had been very worried because she'd had a feeling that her mother was getting sick too. And the very next day Mommy had begun to cough that same terrible croupy cough that Daddy had just before he died. She told Rachel her head and throat hurt. Rachel didn't know what to do, but she did know how to make soup out of melted snow and bits of meat, adding salt and fat, as her mother had taught her. After a feeble attempt to eat the soup Mommy went to bed. Fever wracked her body, just as it had with Daddy. The fever never left her and she grew so weak and worn down that she was unable to get out of bed. And that's where Rachel found her mother that morning, her golden hair matted to her head and her big dark brown eyes closed forever.

Rachel brushed her mother's hair, and then stood by the bed looking at her. She was a beautiful woman. Daddy had often told Rachel that she was the splitting image of her mother. Things that her parents had said and done kept crowding into her mind as she tried to figure out how she was going to move her mother's body. Could she wrap her up like the two of them had wrapped her father? She wanted to do it as well as her mother had done. Rachel pulled the moose hide covering off the bed and laid it on the floor. She then crawled up on the bed, braced her back against the wall, and pushed her mother's body inch by inch with her feet. Finally, Rachel moved off the bed and tried to guide the body down as it dropped onto to the floor. "I'm so sorry Mommy," she cried.

Rachel tugged and pushed and pulled until her mother's body was straight on the hide. Then she took one side of the hide and pulled it around her mother, rolling her with it. It was very hard work, even for a strong girl like Rachel, and beads of sweat dripped off her forehead and ran down into her eyes until she no longer knew whether it was sweat or tears. "Oh Mommy, you're wrapped up snug, just like in a cocoon, she said as she pulled the top part of the hide tenderly down over her mother's beautiful hair.

Rachel stood up slowly, wiping the sweat off her brow with the back of her hand. She scrounged around and found four long strips her father had cut from another hide. Crouching down she laid them out on the floor beside her mother, then rolled her body again until the strips of hide were under her. She wrapped them around her mother's shroud and tied them as tight as she could with the multiple knots her father had taught her. When she was sure everything was as tight and neat as it should be, she laid her head on her mother's chest and wept. Finally, spent from crying, the child fell asleep, exhausted, on the floor.

Upon awakening she resumed her task, trying to

figure out how best to move her mother's body out of the cabin. She got up and slowly pulled her mitts on after deciding that the first thing she must do is dig a hole in the snow like her mother had done for her father. Once the hole was long enough she continued to hollow it until it looked just right. Utterly spent, she sat for some time in the snow and then got up and walked over to the trees where the big black horse was tethered.

Daddy didn't always tether Black. Most of the time he let him roam. After Daddy died Britanny had kept the horse as near as she could. As Rachel walked up to him he started to whicker. He knew there was something terribly wrong and he looked to the little girl for comfort. Looking up at the big horse she felt very small. "Black" … Rachel said … "You have to put your head down. I can't pet you way up there." The big horse put his head down to her small face and she stroked him as he nuzzled her with his soft nose.

Black followed her to the cabin, stopping at the door to see what she wanted to do. Rachel took one end of the long rope she had placed around the horse's neck, and then, opening the cabin door, she bent over her mother and carefully tied the rope around her mother's ankles. "Okay, Black … back … back," she said, as she pushed against his front legs. She had to push with all her might as the top of her head ended where the horse's chest began. As she pushed, Black slowly backed up and her mother's body slid smoothly towards the doorway and through it. Once the body was outside Rachel turned Black around. And then,

talking to the horse all the while, she led him over to
the hollowed-out snow, manoeuvring him so that her
mother was pulled right into the hollow.

Rachel untied the horse and, after a moment or two
of rest, began to pile wood on top of her mother. The
horse seemed to understand and stood by waiting for
her instructions. Once she was done piling a mound
of wood about the same height as her father's mound,
she stood back to look at her work. The sorrow of it all
started to overwhelm her and, sobbing, she slumped
to the ground on her knees. The big black horse stood
over her for a bit, and then started nuzzling at her to
get up. The warm air steaming from his nostrils made
Rachel realize how very cold she was. Shivering, she
pulled herself up from the snow and reached out for
the horse. She gently led him back over to his shelter
in the trees, talking to him the whole time. Rachel
dug around for some meadow hay her father had cut
in the summer and gave several handfuls to the horse
before walking back to the cabin.

As she entered the cabin, she realized her fire had
burnt down to embers. The cabin was cold because
she hadn't shut the door behind her after removing
her mother's body. She stoked the fire again and
looked deep into it for some time. Once it was blazing
she crawled onto the bed and pulled a thick hide over
her. Gradually, the warmth of the cabin dulled her
tired mind and body and she softly cried herself to
sleep.

CHAPTER 2

The Spirit Waif

The Indian camp was in an uproar. Snarling wolves and barking dogs had broken the early morning peace. Now there were dead and injured dogs everywhere. It had been quite a fight and by the looks of things the dogs had lost. An arrow had brought down one lone wolf during the scuffle.

The chief of the tribe, Storm, went looking for the brave who had shot the animal to find out what had happened. He knew it was likely he would get the usual garbled story about a big black horse ridden by a spirit with long white flowing hair, which was accompanied by a pack of wolves. Storm was angry. He didn't believe in spirits, except for those in the ancient tribal realm. He was frustrated with his people because their superstitions seemed to rule their lives. Spirits and ghosts did not steal bags of corn or dried meat, nor did they steal weapons. Humans did these things, not spirits.

Storm's mother was always reminding him that,

after only twenty-five summers, he was young to be a chief. He was a big man, standing six-foot-six, muscular, and narrow in the hips. Storm had piercing black eyes that seemed to look deep into one's soul. His stern facial expressions made others think that he was unapproachable. Many a man had thought twice about facing off with him in a fight. Storm was a formidable foe for anyone who betrayed him. And he never forgave betrayal.

As he strode through the village his anger left him, as he began to realize how upset and unsettled his people were over the early morning events. It saddened him to see the young children crying over their dogs. Storm stopped suddenly when he noticed one dog that was suffering terribly. He immediately pulled the big hunting knife from the sheath that hung around his waist and pierced the dog's heart. Fast Creek, who had been on his way to meet Storm, witnessed this decisive action. Storm was wiping the bloody knife in the grass when Fast Creek reached him.

Even though Fast Creek was a tall man, when he was standing alongside Storm he didn't look that tall. But what Fast Creek had over Storm was his charismatic effect on the young women of his tribe. Storm always wondered how one man could be so attractive to women. All the women in the village vied for his attention, but Fast Creek seemed oblivious to their advances. Storm wondered why he didn't get that kind of attention, never seeming to realize that his arrogant distant nature kept most of his people at bay. This bothered Storm a little but, at the same time, he knew that his men would follow him without question. The entire band liked and respected their serious-minded young chief.

Fast Creek told Storm what had happened that morning. He began by stating, with a self-conscious grin, that he would likely be laughed out of the tribe once his story got around. He had wakened to the barking and snarling of the dogs and had grabbed his bow and arrows on the way out of his teepee, just in time to get knocked off his feet by a huge wolf.

He saw immediately that the dogs didn't stand a chance against the pack of wolves. A couple of the dozen or more wolves were singling dogs out and then taking them down. Fast Creek had watched the action in fascination and disbelief. As the wolves methodically attacked the dogs, he caught sight of the white-haired spirit waif, who had ridden in on the enormous black horse. Fast Creek told Storm that the two seemed like one as they made their way straight for the corn bags. The spirit took but a moment or two and was off in a flash, back onto that horse with two bags of corn, and moving faster than any man he had ever seen.

The second time they came around, Fast Creek raised his bow and fitted an arrow as a wolf came at him from the side. He turned quickly, let the arrow go, and it struck the wolf. By the time he let go with another arrow, the waif and the horse were gone. They vanished like the wind and the rest of the wolves disappeared with them.

Storm listened intently as Fast Creek told him that

they *must* be spirits. How could they disappear before his eyes if they weren't? Storm listened patiently, then said, "Get the horses, we'll track them." As he signalled his men he was already walking toward the horses, calmly issuing orders to the braves.

As they walked past the teepees towards the tethered horses, Storm's eyes opened wide in amazement. The brave who was on lookout was lying motionless on the ground. The horses were gone. The white-haired waif had let the horses loose, and in the panic of the wolf attack they had all run off. It would take some time to round them up. Storm cursed. She had escaped capture again. Just then the sky opened up and it began to rain. The spirits must be with her, he thought, knowing the rain would wash all signs away making it impossible to track her. What he found most unsettling was that she knew exactly where they stored the corn, even though they had recently changed its location. What kind of warriors were they that someone had been able to approach the camp and watch his people without being caught? Storm decided it was time to do something about the situation. This had now happened three autumns in a row.

Storm bent over the brave on the ground. He wasn't dead, but had been knocked unconscious. How could this have happened? He was a big man, as were many of Storm's braves. What, or who, could have gotten close enough to strike the guard that hard without him hearing them coming. Storm vowed to get to the bottom of these strange happenings once and for all.

Rachel knew she was pushing Black. But even after two days on the trail they dared not stop. There was always the possibility that the Indians had picked up her trail in spite of the rain. They were no fools when it came to tracking and she knew it. She walked the horse through several streams to make sure his hoof marks disappeared. The wolves followed her at a distance, only coming in close when she had to stop for a few minutes to give Black a chance to rest. Her heart ached for the pack because she knew they were mourning Thorny as much as she was. How could she have made a mistake like that? The big Indian had almost shot her with his arrow. If Thorny hadn't been protecting her she'd be dead right now.

CHAPTER 3

The Wolf Pack

Rachel felt that familiar lump forming in her throat, and experienced the same sense of loss that had shattered her life when her parents died. Memories washed over her as she rode towards home thinking about the hardships she and Black had endured just to stay alive. Seven years had passed. It seemed a lifetime to Rachel, even though she was now only seventeen.

Her thoughts turned to the pack. They were so much a part of the horse's life, and hers. She thought back to the day she and Black had found those two dead wolves. The wolves were about ten miles from the cabin and had been brought down by arrows. At first glance, Rachel thought it was strange that they had been left to rot rather than skinned for their pelts. It was very unlike the Indians to let anything go to waste. However, on examining the carcasses, she realized the wolves had been wounded and somehow managed to escape, only to die some time later in the underbrush. They had been dead for a day or two when Rachel came across them. As she was examining their bodies she'd heard the faint sound of whimpering and whining, and walked towards the sound. About forty feet from the two dead wolves she found the den, and another dead wolf.

When she kneeled down to look inside the den a little black head poked out, and then another and another until there were six. The last one was pure white and bigger than the rest. At first, Rachel wondered if he was older than the others, but she soon figured he was the same age. But being bigger hadn't made him any more graceful. He was pretty clumsy. The pups, dismissing all caution, rushed out to greet her. They were hungry and lonely, and Rachel figured they must be less than a month old. She walked over to Black and took down the moosehide that was draped over his back. It was a fair-sized hide and served many purposes. The horse was prancing around restlessly. He'd had many run-ins with wolves and he didn't much like them. They smelt odd and he would have liked to trample them with his pitching hooves. Rachel picked the pups up one by one and wrapped them in the hide, leaving an opening so they could breathe. Then she mounted her horse and, with the precious bundle held close, headed for home.

From that moment on, life took on new meaning for Rachel. She took those six little pups home to her cabin, nursing them and training them over the next two or three months. The obedient but playful pups grew quickly and Rachel began to take them hunting. Being natural-born predators, their instinct to hunt was strong and they caught on right away. From their first hunt on, food was no longer an everyday concern for Rachel. When the young wolves brought an animal down and didn't kill it quick enough to suit her, she used her bow and arrow to finish it off. By doing this she was able to save her father's ammunition for times when she really needed it. At Rachel's command the young wolves would obediently sit back and watch her skin the carcass and cut up the meat. They trusted her because they considered her to be their alpha wolf. They seemed to know that when she was finished they would get their share and there would be enough for all of them.

The young wolves were soon well trained and instantly responsive. They knew Rachel's whistle and voice commands, but most of all they reacted to her hand signals and acted on them without a moment's hesitation. Every move she made meant something to the animals, so they watched her carefully. When they arrived back at the cabin after the hunts she would let them roam freely. Although they never strayed too far or for too long, they did have a chance to encounter others of their kind. But when Rachel whistled they would race back to the cabin as fast as their legs could carry them.

It wasn't long before a new litter of pups was born near the cabin. The babies, along with their mother, were immediately moved into the cabin to begin their training. Since wolf pups are always left under the care of other wolves while their mothers hunt for food, the mother wolf willingly let Rachel stay with the pups.

When the pack returned after each hunt the mother would return to the cabin to nurse her babies. Once they were ready for more substantial food she would feed the pups, as all wolves do, with regurgitated food from her stomach. Since this a natural and important survival technique, Rachel never interfered with the feeding of the pups. She knew it was critical that the parents take care of their young.

The wolf pack eventually consisted of a dominant male that Rachel named Shadow and a female she named Ebony. The rest of the pack was submissive first to her, then to Shadow and Ebony. The wolves were big full-bodied animals ranging in colour from grey to black, except for Shadow who was pure white. Ebony was completely black and they made a striking pair.

As Rachel rode Black towards home she glanced around at the pack running beside her, taking in Shadow's magnificent presence as he bounded along. She quickly developed a bond with this huge animal knowing that Shadow, despite his dominance and strength, would be faithful to her under any circumstance. He clearly adored her, and she knew he would lay down his life for her if necessary. Rachel and Black were the only creatures he ever submitted to. Shadow had already been given a few lessons by the horse and knew to watch out for those sharp hooves. But somehow both animals were united in purpose. They each knew, instinctively, that the other was fiercely loyal to the girl in their midst, and they shared and respected the ever-growing bond between the girl and themselves.

Shadow knew that he was king of the pack, even though Rachel reigned over them all when she was around. The girl never interfered with his role. Sometimes a fight would break out and a male wolf, even one she had helped raise since birth, would rebel against submitting to Shadow. The renegade wolf would then be run out of the pack and, although it would break Rachel's heart to lose one of them, there was nothing she could do. It was the law of the land. The wolves that did not submit to the alpha male either left the pack or they died. Shadow's role was not an easy one. There was always a challenger, either within or outside the pack, another great and powerful wolf who lay in wait to take over.

When they approached the last couple of miles around their home territory, the area where the cabin was hidden, Rachel whistled. The pack disappeared into the brush to check if there was any danger lurking. Only Shadow stayed with the horse, and of course Rachel, who was still on his back. Soon there was an enthusiastic howl as Ebony gave the signal that all was clear at the cabin. Over the past seven years dense bush had grown up around the cabin, so perfectly nestled into the riverbank. It was now invisible to passers-by. Only if someone stumbled onto it accidentally would it ever be discovered. Ever since her parents died, Rachel made it a point to vary her route each time she and her animals approached.

As she jumped off Black's back Shadow rubbed up against her. Reaching over she scratched his ears, "Well, we're home boy," she said as she reached up and removed the horse's bridle. Then, slapping his flank, she added, "Go find your herd Black." The great horse had a harem of seventeen mares back in the hills and he'd been away from them for a week. He gave an excited neigh and thundered off into the bush. Rachel never worried about him coming back. If he was within hearing distance of her whistle he'd come as fast as he could, and if he wasn't she would send Shadow to find him. And any time the horse heard the wolf's howl he would immediately head to the cabin to find the girl.

Life was simple for Rachel. Stashing enough firewood and food for the winter was about the only serious challenge. Any time she went away from the cabin she packed deadwood home for the cold months. Finding food wasn't always as easy though. They had to travel further from the cabin than she liked, but she regularly hunted with the pack and they usually got something worthwhile. The berry bushes, the wild roots, and the river in which she fished during those months supplied most of their summer diet. With picking and drying the berries, cleaning and drying the fish, and collecting wild roots and onions the summers passed all too soon. Unfortunately, her favourite foods were the peas and corn she raided from the Indians. She was always hungry for the taste of vegetables.

Rachel had found the Indian village accidentally. About four years earlier she had been so lonesome she set out with Black to find the settlement her father had talked about. But they stumbled on the Indian village instead. The two of them spent almost a week in the area watching the people and studying the layout of the camp. She had seen the fields of corn and peas and had snuck in under the cover of darkness to raid their fields. Rachel watched the women and children at work. Although part of her desperately wanted to approach them, she was careful to remain hidden when the warriors were around. They frightened her because they seemed so serious and foreboding. Usually, when she went to raid the crops in the fall, the braves were away hunting.

This particular year, she had been caught off guard when she approached the camp. Her first mistake had been not checking the camp out. After two previous raids Rachel had become quite confident and had grown a little careless. There was only one brave guarding the horses, so she motioned for Shadow to go to the left of the brave as she moved towards him from the right. Rachel gave a soft whistle when she was in close enough and Shadow vaulted from the semi-darkness knocking the brave down. Even with the air knocked out of him the brave managed to regain his feet and pull his knife from his sheath. Just then Rachel hit him on the back of the head with a heavy stick she had picked up off the ground. But she should have realized by the number of ponies the wolves had chased that the braves were in camp this time.

Of course, she reasoned, they knew by now that she showed up in the fall. Why hadn't she thought of this earlier? Oh well, she would have to suffer the consequences. The thing that really worried her though was that she had lost Thorny. He had been her sentinel wolf and he never left her side. Others went hunting but he was always left to guard his mistress. If she went on the hunt he came but if she stayed home he stayed too.

When she arrived back home and had carefully checked for intruders, she was greeted at the cabin by the two wolves that had remained behind to look after the spring litter of pups. Ebony was overjoyed to see her pups and the two older wolves were happy to run off to join the rest of the pack now that she was back.

Rachel played with the puppies for awhile, amazed at how much they had grown in only a couple of weeks, then picked the bags of corn up from the ground and made her way to the door. After opening the windows she left the door wide open to air the cabin out, and hauled the two bags of corn into the cold room. She heaved a sigh of relief as she noticed that it had started to rain, a welcome reprieve from the heat and dust of their journey.

Rachel whistled and Shadow appeared in the doorway. She gave him a hand signal and he cocked his head from side to side, barked once, and went back outside. From there he gave a couple of sharp barks and the rest of the pack, along with Ebony and the pups, appeared. He gave another yelp and the wolves disappeared into the bush. When they were hunting the pack turned back into the wild animals they were, stalkers and hunters, as nature intended.

CHAPTER 4

The Grizzly Attack

A willow branch snapped across Storm's cheek as he rode through the dense bush and he cussed, reaching up to wipe the blood off his face. Storm wouldn't admit it to anyone but the waif intrigued him. Who was she? Where had she come from? How did she control the wolves and why didn't they rip her apart? And that big black horse ... where had he come from? Storm had seen a wild stallion and his mares in a canyon a few years back, but by the time he got close they had disappeared into another canyon. Could the black horse be that same stallion? And if it was, how could a near-child capture him? Storm decided to search for the girl and the wolves in that same canyon. He figured it must be about two or three days downriver. If he found her he could prove to his tribe, once and for all, that she was flesh and blood and not of the spirit world.

Storm's massive horse, a dune, was very sure-footed. As they picked their way down a steep cliff, he thought about how in tune with each other they were.

He knew he could depend on this horse. But the girl and her horse were beyond being in tune, they had an uncanny relationship.

Rachel stayed around the cabin for a week, fishing and collecting firewood. Even the wolves helped, bringing all manner of sticks into the camp and dropping their offerings at her feet. By late fall she had quite a stash of wood, certainly enough for the winter. Nevertheless, she continued to pick up more whenever she left the camp.

Any time loneliness set in Rachel unconsciously began to whistle. She hadn't seen the wolves or the horse for a week and wondered where they all were and what they were doing. The thought had no sooner crossed her mind than she saw Shadow coming toward her through the trees. Following close behind were Wind and Bullet. In the next moment, there were wolves behind her. As she slowly reached back, Cloud put his big head under her hand. They began to gather around her, but as Shadow came in closer they backed off a bit. They knew his jealous ways. Shadow thought he was the only one in her life and was very possessive. Of course, none of them would dare challenge him. Even Ebony had to stay back until Shadow greeted Rachel. She put her face into his fur and hugged him to her, and then she gave the signal for the wolf to go find Black. Shadow turned to go, threw his big head back, and let out a howl that sent shivers down Rachel's spine. She loved that howl, and she knew that within an hour or two the horse would show up.

Rachel and Black moved though the great pines. It was breathtakingly beautiful in the thick of the trees. Six wolves weaved in and out of the bush with them, sometimes chasing squirrels, chipmunks, and birds. If they really got lucky a rabbit would cross their path and a real chase would begin. Never venturing far, they came back every few minutes to trot quietly beside the big horse and his rider. As they rode Rachel noticed grizzly markings on several trees. A big one, she thought. His reach was as high on the tree as she was on the back of the horse. A little unnerved, she told Black that she wouldn't want to meet up with this one. But she knew it was highly unlikely because if she were ever in danger, the wolves would sense the bear's presence and warn her.

As they cleared the trees they came to the top of a hill. After a moment or two she got off the horse scanned the valley below. Startled, she saw a lone rider off in the distance heading north towards the hill. An Indian. What was he doing here? This was highly unusual as he was completely alone. She watched him for the better part of an hour. He moved slowly and deliberately, often looking down at the ground and stopping now and then. He was definitely looking for something, but what? As Rachel watched and waited the grizzly came into sight some distance below in the valley. She watched the bear and the Indian as they unknowingly headed towards each other. Or so she thought. Her demeanour changed from one of curious observer to one of a helpless bystander when she realized they were getting closer and closer to each other. Rachel was amazed that the horse didn't catch the scent of the bear and rear up in warning. She soon realized that a fairly strong wind was blowing from the west and this meant that neither horse nor bear would have much warning.

Rachel suddenly grew concerned when she realized the grizzly knew exactly where the horse was. The two were on a collision course and the grizzly was clearly intent on attacking the horse. Stopping every so often, it stood on his hind legs and sniffed the air. By the time the horse recognized the danger it would be too late, the bear would be on top of them. There was no use yelling, as the rider couldn't possibly hear her over the wind from this distance. Rachel, now fully alarmed, dispersed the wolves. Shadow, who had been watching the bear intently, growled deep in his throat as Rachel gave the command to attack. In no time the pack disappeared from view. She hurriedly mounted her horse, knowing the wolves could run faster through the trees than Black, and hoping that they would make it in time to ward off the bear or at least help to prevent the attack.

Storm had been dozing on his horse as he'd been riding a long time and the heat had made him feel sleepy. Suddenly, the grizzly stood up right in front of him. The horse tried to rear up but was too late. The bear reached out with his great claws, swiped the horse across the neck and ripped its throat open. Storm flew through the air and landed face down on the ground. Gasping for air, he turned on his side and reached for his knife while trying to regain his feet.

Just as the knife cleared the sheath the grizzly was upon him. The man felt the claws go deep into his back, and as the bear bit down on his head let out a blood-curdling scream. Blinded by searing pain he stabbed wildly with his knife as the bear rolled him over. Storm was going to die and he knew it. The last thing he saw before blacking out was a massive white wolf flying through the air at the bear.

As Shadow struck from the front, the grizzly turned. Cloud came in on him from behind. Wind and Bolt flew at the bear's left and right side just Ebony and Salt joined Shadow in front of the man. The grizzly turned around and around in confusion as the wolves kept up their attack. One swipe across Bolt's shoulder sent him flying through the air into the trunk of a tree.

Rachel and Black appeared just as the grizzly bolted and crashed into the bush with the pack close on his heels. Rachel sucked in her breath as she watched them go for the grizzly. By now she could see his distinctive marking. It was the killer bear, and he was still alive. No wonder it had attacked. It had caught its prey's scent from a long way off and had been following the man on the horse. Rachel jumped off Black and ran to the wolf on the ground. Kneeling beside him she rolled him over, he was badly clawed on the shoulder and the wind had been knocked out of him. She thought she might be able to sew him together if she could just get him home.

She then turned her attention to the man on the ground. The sight was overwhelming. There was blood everywhere. He was laying half on his side and half on his stomach. The skin on his back was peeled right down to his waist and the side of his face was open to the bone. His hair was matted with blood and his wounds were pulsating more blood onto the ground. As she tried to straighten him out his left arm dangled limply.

After quickly pulling a moosehide from her horse's back, she used her knife to cut it into strips and then placed a large piece of it over the Indian's back. Shuddering, she saw that the open wound was filled with dirt and debris. Rachel tied the strips of rawhide together, and then forced them under the man who was by now lying on his stomach. She struggled to put strips of hide under him, and then tie each one of them at the man's side in order to secure the big piece over his wound. By this time his arm was out of its socket. Pulling with all her might, she felt his shoulder pop back in and thought she was going to be sick. It was only sheer force of will that enabled her to carry on. She quickly cut another long rawhide strip from the hide. Winding this completely around him, she forced his arm to bend and tied it tight against his body. With great effort she then turned him back onto his stomach, to get him off his torn-up back. She knew she had to get him back to the cabin or he was not going to survive. Rachel picked up his hatchet, which was lying beside his dead horse.

The young girl then began the arduous job of cutting small willows down to make a *travois* to carry him home. Although she had never made one before, she had seen drawings in a book. She knew that the Indians used them for pulling things around. Even if Black were to lie down beside him, she would never be able to get his big body on her horse. Once the saplings were ready she began cutting the remaining leather into strips so she could tie the willows together at the four corners. Then she tied four strips close together down the middle. She looked at Black and what was left of the hide she carried. There was no way she had enough hide or strips to make a proper travois, but she used what was left to put over the frame she had made. Poking holes through the edges of the hide with her knife, she then ran strips through to tie the hide to the frame so it wouldn't pull off. Looking around for something more to use, she focused on the man's horse. She would be able to use the reins, his horse blanket, and his bedroll.

The wolves weren't back yet, so she whistled them in. A few minutes later they appeared at her side, panting laboriously. She quickly looked Shadow over to make sure he had not been seriously hurt, and then motioned him to her side. She tied strips of blankets around Shadow's back and belly, fastened long strips on each side of Shadow, and tied them to the travois. It wasn't a very good travois but she hoped it would stay together until they made it home. Once the hide was secure across the poles she hacked off boughs from the poplar trees and laid them on the makeshift stretcher.

The task was now to roll the man onto it. The heat of the day and the strain of pushing and pulling were taking its toll, and Rachel was getting weaker by the moment. With the last of her energy she slowly rolled him onto the travois, then motioned Shadow over to Bolt, who was still lying where she had left him. She half-packed and half-dragged Bolt onto the injured man. She knew there was no way Black would carry the wolf unless she too was riding. But Rachel couldn't mount the horse because she had to stay on the ground to help Shadow pull the travois. When everything was secured she got behind Shadow, gripping both the poles so she could help him pull. The combined weight of the man and the wolf was almost three hundred and fifty pounds.

The trip back to the cabin was slow going. The wolf and the girl stopped often to rest. They had travelled about a mile when Rachel knew for certain that she and Shadow could never pull that much weight so far. She would either have to make two trips, or she would have to talk her horse into carrying the wolf. Black, who was following along beside them, nickered when she called him to her. "Black you're going to have to help me. Please carry Bolt." Then, bringing the horse in nearer to the makeshift travois Rachel motioned the horse to lie down close to the travois. Black didn't like it and lunged to his feet knocking her down. She jumped to her feet and gave him a sharp smack on the soft part of his jaw. Black was stunned. Rachel had never before slapped him. Standing there he began to tremble until she began talking to him calmly and soothingly.

Gently, she coaxed him to lie down again. Then, reaching across him she tried to pull Bolt across his back but couldn't do it. She thought for a moment and then cut up the horsetail reins, which were still on the Indian's horse, and tied them tightly together. One end she tied around Bolt's middle and the other around Salt's chest. When she had everything in place she coaxed Salt to pull with her. Inch by inch they managed to pull the wolf off the man on the travois and onto the horse's back. Then, carefully hanging onto the wolf, Rachel got Black to stand up. Snorting he began prancing around until she yelled at him. If he dumped the wolf back on the ground she would have to leave him for a second trip. But just as suddenly as the horse had acted up he settled down, seeming to realize Rachel needed him. Stroking Black she said soothingly, "I need you to do this boy. You know if there was another way I wouldn't ask you."

Then she went calmly back to Shadow, stepped in behind him, picked up the bindings that were still free, and began to pull. What a difference it made dragging the man without the wolf. When they were about an hour from the cabin, Rachel motioned Cloud in and untied Shadow who immediately laid down to rest. She knew if she kept him on the travois he'd pull until he dropped. Once she got Cloud tied to the travois in Shadow's place, she threw herself down to rest beside Shadow. Ebony crowded her on the other side. The wolves were panting and everyone needed a drink of water. Near exhaustion herself, she slowly heaved herself up off the ground. She didn't even glance at the Indian when they resumed their trek resignedly. If he died he died, there was nothing more she could do to help him.

They arrived home in the early evening. Rachel didn't stop at the cabin, but headed straight to the river and stopped near some trees. From there she got the horse to lie down again, and with considerable effort pulled Bolt off his back, telling them both that she'd be right back. She hugged Black and he immediately lunged back onto his hooves. He couldn't help prancing around, he was so glad to get that wolf off of his back. "You're a good boy," she told him. Then she signalled Cloud to pull the travois into the river. Once the man's body was under the water with only his head out, she propped a rock under the front of the travois. This kept his head above water until she freed Cloud from the makeshift stretcher. She then walked into the river for a long slow drink of water, splashing her grimy face and neck at the same time. After resting for some time, Rachel began to think about what she had to do next. The Indian was still unconscious, but he was alive. That was a good thing because what she had to do next would be very painful.

Rachel left the river and went to the cabin to see what she could find in her mother's big box. In it, among other things, were sinew, a bone needle, and an assortment of clean rags. She made a fire, put water on to boil, and then added the rags to the boiling water. In the cold storage room, she scrounged around until she found some mould and scraped it up to take back to the fire. Then, after putting another pot of water on the fire, she threw the mould into it and lay down for a few minutes. Her father had told her that mould, when made into a tea with various herbs, helped to get rid of an infection. And infection killed more people than anything else in those days, as even a small cut or scratch often result in blood poisoning.

When Rachel had everything ready she packed it all down to the river. She untied the hide patch she had put over the brave's back and let the fast-moving river wash against the open wound while she rinsed off the moosehide patch. The river cleaned the dirt and debris out of the mangled flesh. Then she carefully shifted her patient to protect his back from the rough travois, and signalled Shadow back into the river. She tied him once again to the travois and she and Shadow pulled it from the river. By this time there was very little light left in the sky so Rachel had to move quickly. She rolled him onto the moosehide, and left him on his stomach. She gagged as she pulled the skin together on his back. The bear's claws had gone in so far that Rachel could see muscle and ribs. She began to sew the skin, stitch after stitch. When she was finished the stitches formed a huge horseshoe shape on his back.

By this time, darkness was descending so she moved quickly to pour the mould and herbs onto his back. Then, with some difficulty, she wrapped the boiled rags around him, pushing and pulling until she got them in place over the terrible wound. Once she was done she rolled him onto his side and started on his face. His cheekbone was protruding through the skin, so she carefully pressed the skin down the best she could over the hole left by the bear's claws. Near exhaustion, she started stitching again, closing up with whatever skin she could get hold of. His nose was broken so she forced it back into position. The grizzly had done most of his work on the man's head, and she wasn't sure whether or not his skull was fractured.

Anything other than sewing the skin together was well beyond Rachel's skill and knowledge. The bear's teeth had made deep puncture wounds and the man's hair was caught up in his wounds. After she had stitched everything she could, she checked his arm and thought it best to leave it tied to his body. When she was done that she tucked a moosehide around him and covered him with an additional hide to protect him from the chill of the coming night. His body was cold from the river and the night air. She had done all she could for him, and now the only thing that could make a difference was his will to live.

Rachel hooked Shadow to the travois and motioned him over to Bolt. She loaded the wolf onto the travois and added all the other things she had brought from the cabin. Last of all, she motioned for Ebony to stay and guard the man for the night.

Back at the cabin she lit a candle and worked long into the night stitching Bolt's wounds closed. At one point she cried when Bolt whined in pain. Although he seemed to know she was helping him, he came close to biting the hand that was causing him so much pain. Finally, when she was through working on the wolf and had cleaned up the mess, she threw some meat out to the pack. It had gone rancid from the heat but this made it all the more appealing for the wolves. She noticed that the whole pack had come home. They were all waiting to see how Bolt was making out.

Rachel left the cabin door open so they could come and go as they pleased. Some came up and sniffed Bolt while others lay down beside him. She got another hide and then she too lay down on the floor next to the wolf. As Rachel floated off to sleep the last thing she remembered seeing through her tired burning eyes was Shadow. His huge white body loomed over her and the downed wolf, protecting them as they slept.

CHAPTER 5

A Difficult Patient

Rachel was awakened in the morning by a slobbery but gentle kiss across her eyes and nose. She opened her eyes and looked into Bolt's furry face. After she kissed the end of his nose he turned and limped to the door. There were no other wolves in sight but when he whined pitifully, three of them appeared out of nowhere to keep him company. Rachel got up, lit a fire, and put the kettle on to boil. She then washed up with some of the warm water. As she brushed her long white hair and braided it back behind her head she thought that she and Shadow must be kindred spirits because her hair was almost the colour of his fur.

Once she had enough water boiling she strained the mould she had prepared the night before, and when only mould remained she put it into fresh boiling water. It was very bitter, even when the herbs were added, so she put a little honey in to sweeten it. She poured the mixture into a bowl containing ground corn cooked into a mush and mixed them

41

both together. Next, she removed the rags she had boiled in the second pot and placed them in her water bucket. Then she left the cabin with her bucket and started down the trail to the river, wondering if the Indian was still alive. As she entered the clearing Ebony came to meet her, and she patted the wolf on the head telling her she was good girl. Rachel gave Ebony a piece of meat she had brought for her. The wolf gulped the meat down, waited for Rachel's command, and then disappeared into the bush.

Rachel walked over to the wounded man, "So you're still alive." If anything his face looked worse than the night before. It was so swollen and bruised it was grotesque. Rachel knew he was no threat to her. He was so weak from loss of blood that only his eyes moved when she knelt down beside him on the ground. As she lifted his head to feed him the mould and corn mush he moaned in agony. She put her hand on his forehead and determined he was feverish. Rachel gave a whistle, and in a few minutes Shadow appeared at her side. The wolf watched her as she unwrapped the bandages from the night before. What a mess his body was, blood everywhere. Rachel put a moosehide on the travois and rolled him over. She knew it hurt him, but she didn't have any choice because he couldn't help her at all.

Once he was on the travois Rachel tied Shadow to it so he could pull the man into the river again. She put him in deep enough so that she could roll him off his back onto his good side, trying to make sure his face wasn't in the water. At one point, when she let go of the travois to set Shadow free, his whole head momentarily slipped under the water. As their eyes met she saw panic in his eyes.

Rachel let the cold running water of the river sooth his wounds and wash out any dirt still embedded in his flesh. Then she left him in the water for a few minutes, thinking this might reduce his fever. When she was satisfied he'd been in the water long enough, she got Shadow to pull him from the river and take him over to the clean hide she had placed in the grass. Rachel rolled him off the travois onto his side and then, with his good side down, she pushed him onto his stomach so she could work on his back again. She patted his body dry and, trying not to hurt him, very carefully applied bear grease to his wounds. Once that was done she bandaged his body and head, rolled him back on his side, and proceeded to feed him the mush. He didn't want to eat but she held his head up and encouraged him. He had no choice but to swallow, gagging several times because of the terrible taste. This took patience. Nevertheless, she persevered, knowing that it probably did taste pretty bad. At least she had managed to feed him and at the same time had got medicine into him.

When all this was finished she slowly coaxed two small cups of water into him, thinking that it might help to replenish the blood in his body. It was obvious he was low on blood as his brown skin was very pale. Rachel then covered him with a clean hide and left him to sleep in the warm sun. And by the time she had washed the other moosehide in the river and hung it to dry he was either in a very deep sleep or unconscious, she wasn't sure which.

Wind appeared out of the bush as soon as Rachel bid him with a sharp whistle. His hair stood up on his neck because he didn't recognize the smell of this man, and was understandably leery as he came toward the girl. She motioned for the wolf to lay down close the man and to guard him, freeing Shadow so he could go off to hunt. Rachel took one last look at the man. She didn't think he'd make it through the day, but she had done what she could.

Storm woke some time later trying to recall where he was and why. He turned his head slightly ... and looked straight into the eyes of the huge wolf lying beside him. Terror seized him as the wolf stared at him without blinking. Storm tried to move his body away but he was unable to because of the searing pain that racked him when he moved. The wolf closed its eyes. Nothing happened. He was conscious that his lips were cracked and dry, and he was extremely thirsty. The sound of running water in the river didn't help the situation. Storm's thoughts turned to the girl who had been attending him. So this was the spirit waif that had his band spooked. He was surprised how strong she was. He'd thought she was going to drown him but she had managed to keep his face free of the water, most of the time. It was obvious she was hard headed and she seemed to have no fear. The girl didn't seem to care if he groaned or screamed when she took the bandages off. She didn't show any emotion as she tugged and pushed him into the river. He knew by this time that when he fevered up again, that's where he was going to go, whether he liked or not. He was convinced he was going to freeze to death as she always ignored his pleas for help. She wanted him to soak for a set length of time and that was that.

The girl had removed his pants because it was easier for her to tend to his wounds and to help him when he had to relieve himself. Strangely enough, she seemed to sense when he was ready. He avoided looking her in the face whenever she helped him with this. Aside from being completely naked, he was humiliated because he had never been so helpless, at least not since he was a baby being carried around by his mother. Now, suddenly, there was a woman doing everything for him, and a white one at that.

Each time she was done bathing him she'd rub bear grease on him and bandage him up. Then she'd force him to move. He couldn't believe how much pain he was experiencing. It was beyond anything he had ever imagined. Then there was that disgusting tea ... just thinking about it made him shudder. At these times he could only move his head from side to side in an attempt to escape her determined grasp. He knew he was acting like a hysterical child but he couldn't stop himself. She got around his squirming and struggling by sitting on the ground and trapping his head between her surprisingly strong legs. She'd then pinch his cheeks together, forcing him to open his mouth. The next thing he knew she was pouring tea down his throat. He had to admit it. She didn't lose her patience with him often, even when he was struggling like a child. But his embarrassment knew no bounds. He couldn't protect himself at all, as even the slightest movement sent pain ripping through his head and back. Occasionally, he could move his good arm slightly, but that was a feat that made him realize just how weak he really was.

When a week had passed and he hadn't died, Rachel knew the mould tea was working. But what a fight she'd had with the big Indian to take it. Didn't he know she was trying to help him? When she thought he was recovered enough to eat a little, she made him some soup with meat cut into small pieces, to which she had added wild onions, peas, and corn. It tasted pretty good and it was the first real food he'd had in the week he was with her. She had kept him on the tea and ground corn broth, with honey added to both. Sometimes she thought he really disliked her, as anger always flared across his face when she forced him into things he didn't want to do. She could tell that he was a very proud man and that not too many people had ever made him do something he didn't want to do. Well, there was a first time for everything she thought, smugly enjoying the moment. It made her feel powerful and in control. But even so, Rachel was surprised to discover that a big man like this could act so childish.

By the time Rachel got over her musing and headed down to the river her patient was awake. Wind was lying there staring at him and it was obvious that the wolf unnerved the man. Rachel walked over and felt his head. He jerked away from her touch and scowled at her. For the first time since she had started caring for him she laughed out loud. Storm's mouth dropped open. He liked the sound of her laughter and for the first time it dawned on him that she was beautiful.

One day when she was feeding him, he suddenly yelled out that he did not like the "slop." It was Rachel's turn to be surprised. "You speak English?" she asked, incredulously. He told her, haltingly, that he'd learned it from the "black robes."

"Well, I'm sorry you don't like it but you must keep on taking it," she replied. "It stops you from getting infection. But if you want to get blood poisoning and die, that's up to you," she said sarcastically. "Since I know you can speak English, you can make your own decisions from now on. Do you know how to make other medicines that taste better? You can teach me about them."

Storm asked if she was going to put him in the river again. "Of course," she replied, "I need to change the bandages every day and boil them to disinfect them. We must keep every thing clean, especially the wounds on your back. In some places there wasn't even enough skin to stitch together. The wounds are open and they're deep." Communication between them required quite a bit of pantomime and talking with their hands.

"Today, I'm going to untie your arm to see if you can move it. You have to start moving it or it might lock in that position." She removed the sling and he groaned as she tried to straighten his arm out. But that didn't stop her. Each time she moved his arm it pulled on his back, and it hurt. She moved his arm up and down gently; watching his face closely and only stopping when she saw beads of sweat break out on his forehead. Then she removed the hide from him taking absolutely no notice of his nakedness. He was mortified not to have any clothes on, especially in front of a woman.

Rachel rolled him onto the travois, motioned for Wind to come in close, and hooked the wolf up to it. At her signal the animal pulled Storm into the river. When Storm was reasonably comfortable and settled in the water he asked her, "What do they call you?" She told him her name was Rachel and asked what his name was. She noted the pride in his voice as he spoke his name ... "Storm." Rachel had already been thinking that he must be someone of considerable importance in his tribe. By the way he talked to her, she had been sure that he was used to issuing orders and to being obeyed.

Once he was out of the water, dried, greased, and wrapped she came at him with the mouldy-tasting tea. As usual he gagged as he swallowed it. Rachel quickly handed him a drink of water and then began to feed him the soup. He seemed to like it. He ate all of it in addition to the cornmeal biscuits she had baked and spread with honey.

Rachel asked him if he wanted to lie on his other side or on his stomach. He indicated his stomach and she said, "Do you think you could use your legs and help me roll you over? I don't want to hurt your back any more than I have to." Things were much easier now that they could communicate. She put her hands on his shoulders and used all her strength to push him bit by bit until he was on his stomach. Then she covered him with the moosehide. He was very quiet and all the colour had left his face. She knew he was in agony. He looked like he was going to be sick and he tried to hide it from her as he retched. Storm was still extremely weak and he looked just awful.

For three weeks Rachel cared for the Indian during the day, and at night Wind came in to protect him. She intentionally left Wind with this task so that Storm would only become familiar with one wolf, and not the whole pack. When more than one wolf was around Storm became waspish and belligerent. If he was afraid of the great creature he hid it quite well. At the end of the second week she told him she had to take the stitches out of his back and head. Storm protested, cursing. Sometimes he was convinced that she was bent on finishing him off.

Rachel used her knife to remove all the sinew. She worked slowly but surely, telling him all the while how good she thought his wounds looked. Once that ordeal was done with, she fed him again and said to him, "I'll let you rest today, but tomorrow we will be going into deeper water where you're going to walk and move your body. A few days after that, if you are strong enough, we will try walking on land."

As she gathered up the stuff to pack back to the cabin Bolt wandered into the clearing. The wolf eagerly came over to stand by her and, as she ran her hands over his body, she told the wolf, "I might as well remove your stitches too." Storm watched in utter amazement as she cut the stitches out of the wolf's shoulder. He asked her if Bolt was one of the wolves that attacked the bear and saved his life. "Yes," said Rachel, "And you are lucky he didn't die." Storm asked why this made him lucky and she replied, sucking him right in, "If the wolf had died I would have left you to die too."

Taking her quite literally, Storm couldn't believe his ears. No one had every dared to talk to him like this. She watched his reaction as his demeanour turned hostile. His dark brown eyes turned black and stormy. How dare she talk to him as if she were his equal? This woman-child was really pushing her luck. Women did not speak to him unless he spoke to them first. In his village women were expected to remain silent in his presence. Of course, that was an accepted part of the courting game among his people. Being their chief, most young maidens hoped that he might notice or acknowledge them. Yet this young girl didn't seem to care whether he talked to her or not.

In fact, this bold and arrogant one cut him off in mid-sentence when he asked questions she didn't want to answer. Storm was very upset by her aggressive manner and her assumption that she could just drop into his life and take charge. Didn't she know she was insulting him? And didn't she know her place as a woman? He wondered what kind of upbringing she'd had. Probably brought up by wolves, he sneered to himself. He closed his eyes in a lame attempt to convince her that he was asleep. That should be a hint that he wanted to be left alone. He would tolerate her attentions when he was good and ready and not before.

Rachel chuckled. She always knew when he was frustrated with her. He acted so childish if he didn't get his own way or if she chose to disagree with him. His anger didn't bother her one bit. If he thought for a moment that he was more important to her than her wolves ... well ... he wasn't. If Bolt had died fighting that grizzly she would have left him there to die. Or would she? She was being ridiculous. Of course she would have left him. He meant nothing to her.

As she cleaned up the mess and got ready to leave, Storm suddenly opened his eyes and asked her when she was going to move him to her lodge. Rachel looked at him through narrowed eyes and didn't answer. She had no intention of showing him where her cabin was, not now, not ever. When she had hauled him home and down to the river he had been unconscious. He had no idea where he was. Each time she left him she went the same way into the bush, but once out of sight she backtracked different ways to the cabin. Besides, it was at least half-a-mile from where he was lying by the river. Storm watched the look on her face and knew he had pushed her too far. She does a good job of hiding her emotions, Storm noted, as she sullenly walked away from him. In the beginning, he had pompously believed that he could talk her into showing him where her lodge was. This girl had a mind of her own, and a determination he had never seen in a woman before. It made him angry, but it also intrigued him.

The next day Rachel, towing her axe and a couple of extra hides, arrived at the river earlier than usual. She was aware that Storm was watching her as she set about cutting down small trees. When she had enough of them cut she started to make a lean-to. She knew that the mild weather wasn't going to hold forever. Sooner or later it was gong to start raining again and her patient would need shelter. When she was done with the frame she laid pine branches over the top to keep out the weather. She then hung the moosehides over the opening. She knew Storm would be safe inside from predators, especially with Wind watching over him at night.

Storm watched her work and observed that she was quite capable of doing almost anything physical. He thought about her reaction to his question about the cabin. He realized his approach had backfired and had spurred her into immediate action. She had that lean-to up and ready for occupancy faster than he'd ever seen. Storm scowled at her. She had gotten the best of him and he knew it. She knew it too and this did not please him at all.

When the structure was finished, Rachel's attention turned to Storm. As she began to take the hide off his body the sight of his nakedness suddenly embarrassed her. She didn't 't understand why she felt the way she did. His broad shoulders and chest narrowed down to his hips and she was fascinated by his arousal, which was obvious in his eyes as well as the significant physical change. She was more than a little shocked by the process. Rachel had never seen a naked man before Storm, and her cheeks suddenly reddened. To cover her feeling of confusion, she tried to hide her face with her hair and began to whistle, which brought Shadow out of the thick trees.

This particular wolf intimidated Storm and he didn't really know why. Perhaps it was the uncanny relationship between the wolf and the girl. It was clear that the wolf adored this slight but powerful woman-child. Storm was amazed to see the wolf jump up on Rachel and rest his paws on her shoulders, his head well above hers. The animal licked the girl's face and she wrapped her arms affectionately around his huge neck. The wolf dwarfed her in size. Storm was impressed. As he watched the wolf with the girl he knew, without a doubt, that any living being who hurt this girl would die or the wolf would die protecting her. His devotion to her was puzzling but fascinating. Storm watched as the wolf lay down on the ground on his back to show his submission to her. Storm had noticed that when the other wolves were around they submitted to the big white wolf. This was the alpha wolf, no doubt about it, except when it came to the girl. And he was not just submissive to her; he was completely under her spell. Storm had never seen anything between a human and an animal that was anywhere near this relationship.

By this time, Rachel had hooked the wolf to the travois and the Indian was unceremoniously being dragged into the water. This time it was unnerving.

The big wolf didn't stop in the shallow water but pulled with great and sudden force until he was swimming. What made the wolf do this? Then suddenly, out of nowhere, the young girl was pulling on Storm's shoulder … pulling him under the water. Rage filled Storm. Was she trying to drown him? As he was struggling to hold his breath, he felt her come alongside of him. With one swift motion she roughly shoved him off the travois and adeptly pulled his head up to break the surface of the water. Taking great gulps of air he cursed at her.

So, just to spite him, she pushed his head back under the water again. Rachel felt him tremble and she knew it wasn't fear. He was in a rage, and she figured that if he weren't so helpless he would have hit her. Then, it was Rachel's turn to shudder as she looked into the fury of his piercing black eyes. Storm saw Shadow swim away from him and realized he had better try to move his stiff resisting limbs or he would drown. He felt lame and sluggish and couldn't believe the weakness that overwhelmed him. Rachel was there beside him, and that's when he began to realize that the deep water gave him a sensation of freedom and lightness. In the next moment he noticed that she was floating along beside him, holding him up. She guided him to where he could feel the bottom of the river with his feet. "Move your legs!" Rachel shouted, and his legs automatically started to pump. Then she hollered, "Now move your arms!" He didn't respond, so she pushed him back deeper into the river and moved away from him. Automatically his arms came up and he began to move. He roared with the pain. For a few moments it completed consumed him. He had been lying for three weeks in one place and every fibre of his body was protesting. Beads of sweat broke out over his brow, even in the coolness of the water, but his arms and legs were moving together for the first time since the bear's attack. The wrenching pain in his back was beginning to subside — and he passed out with that thought on his mind.

When he awoke he was back on land lying on the moosehide. It wasn't possible. He must have been dreaming. How did she get him out of the river? There was no way she could have dragged him from the water to the hide. He looked at the wolf that was sitting beside him. "I owe you again," he said weakly, putting his hand out to the wolf. Shadow rolled back his lip and bared his teeth, pulling back from the hand reaching out to him. Then he got up and walked over to the girl who was also lying on the ground. Storm smiled inside, with the corner of his mouth twitching at the wolf. I won't make that mistake again he thought, I could have lost my hand.

Rachel had already been extremely tired when Storm lost consciousness in the water. Still, she had held him up until Shadow swam awkwardly back out to her. This wasn't easy for the wolf as he was still tied to the travois. When he finally came alongside her, Rachel used the last of her strength to place Storm's arms over Shadow's back. She held on to his hands from the front to keep him there. Shadow put all his strength into swimming, hindered by the big Indian on his back and the travois dragging along behind them. Rachel was balancing Storm the best she could in the water. Once they were near shore she painstakingly rolled him back onto the travois. It was a good thing he didn't regain consciousness until she had him settled on the dry hide. By the time she put the clean bandages on the man he was in a deep sleep. The ordeal had taken its toll on his pain-wracked and weakened body.

Every day Rachel took him into the water, and with each new day Storm regained more of his strength. When he felt his strength returning, he told her he wanted to try walking on the ground and leaning on her, instead of going in the water. She agreed and helped him to sit up. She tried to help him stand but this was too difficult for both of them. Rachel whistled for Shadow and then directed the wolf to stand in front of the man. She told Storm to hold on tight to Shadow's fur and pull himself up. Meanwhile, she positioned herself behind Storm and put her arms under his to help with the lift. Storm hesitated. The last time he had reached out to this animal he had almost lost his hand. Now she wanted him to pull on his fur!

"This can not be done," Storm said, refusing to reach out to the wolf. Rachel calmly replied, "He won't hurt you because he knows I want him to help you. But don't ever touch him unless I tell you to. If you do, he will kill you." Suddenly, Storm lost his temper and thundered at her, "How does *he* know that! By you moving your head? Not possible." Rachel glared back, "Exactly. The wolf knows."

Still, Storm sat there while the wolf waited patiently. She asked him what the problem was now. Finally, Rachel began to get red. Her face felt like it was on fire. The Indian was stark naked and he knew in an instant what she was feeling. Not a word was exchanged between them. She quickly looked away from his smouldering eyes.

Confused, she felt like she was being sucked into the depth of his soul. She was wondering what on earth had come over her. With her heart beating hard against her ribcage, she picked up a good-sized piece of deerskin and handed it to him. She was sure he could hear her heart thumping. "Wrap this around you I'll turn away," she said.

Storm didn't say anything but inside he was jubilant. He had finally broken through to her. It was the first time he had seen her demonstrate any emotion towards him. She usually appeared haughty or indifferent. It was comforting to know that he wasn't the only one was being betrayed by his body. How many times had she touched him, making his body quiver? He had been humiliated when his body hardened and he could do nothing about it. Maybe now she would find something for him to wear. He did realize that she really hadn't any choice but to keep him naked. There had been no way to avoid the problem, as he had not been able to do anything by himself. But now that he was able to stand and walk on his own he desperately wanted to be clothed.

Storm got his mind back to the task at hand and concentrated on pulling on the wolf's fur. Rachel helped to lift him by putting her arms around his chest and pulling upwards while he staggered to his feet. The wolf let Storm lean fully on him, and the man marvelled at how huge and how strong this giant of a wolf was. Rachel, meanwhile, still had her arms around him supporting him. Slowly, he was aware that the heat of his body was blending with hers. Rachel was feeling strange too, a little light-headed and her hands were quivering. What was happening to her? Storm could feel her hands quivering. He closed his eyes, suddenly hungry for the feeling of a woman's body against him. But he fought the urge to turn and take her into his arms. Instead, he gruffly said, "Let me go now. And come around to my side so I can lean on you."

Rachel moved to his side as if in a trance and he put his good arm around her leaving the weaker one on the back of the wolf. The wolf and Rachel walked Storm around the clearing. He moved very slowly but steadily and after resting briefly against a tree, he came back to rest on the moosehide. As he tried to sink smoothly down onto the moosehide his knees buckled and he fell in an awkward heap. He was exhausted. Patiently, he waited for her to cover him. But she left him uncovered, walked over to the bundle on the ground, and pulled out a large pair of pants. Storm said, "Why did you not give me the pants before I walked?" Rachel quietly replied, "I had to see if you could stand or walk a bit on your own first." They were both very quiet for some time while he rested. After a long time, without either of them saying a word, she took the pants over to him and helped him put them on.

Storm asked where she got the pants and she told him that they were her father's clothes. He asked her where her father was and she told him matter-of-factly that her father and mother were dead. He began to ask her another question but she turned her back and walked away from him.

As he lay there in the sunshine Storm felt surprisingly good and, for the first time in weeks, he was pleased with himself.

Another week passed. One morning she appeared as usual, but this time there were six wolves on her heels, some Storm had seen before, but others were new to him. He looked at her with questioning eyes. Rachel said, "We are taking you back to your village soon." Storm's heart jumped in his chest.

He was sure his tribe had thought him dead when he did not return to the village. If they had believed he was alive, they would have found him by now. Or would they? He also couldn't believe that he and his men had not be able to find the waif either, after looking for her each fall for three years. They had searched long and hard for her. Where did she hide? Did she even have a lodge? Maybe she lived in a cave with the wolves. He didn't believe this was possible but then maybe it was. Wait until his people heard that she had found him first.

CHAPTER 6

Unfamiliar Stirrings

Storm was now at the stage where he could walk a short distance by himself. He had tried to follow Rachel once but had been turned back by one of the wolves, which stopped and held fast to the invisible trail. It looked like he wasn't going to get a chance to find her dwelling.

A few days later, without any warning, Rachel got the travois ready for the trip. When she whistled a number of wolves appeared, some with loaded packs on their backs. And to Storm's amazement, the big black stallion thundered in shortly after another beckoning whistle. Storm's eyes widened as the huge animal slowed and pranced up to the child-like woman. Rachel calmly backed the horse up to the travois and ran straps down to the conveyance from his back. It was going to be a long hard trip she knew that, strong as he was, Shadow could not pull the Indian very far. They needed the great strength of the big black horse.

Storm noticed a large knife around her waist, the bow and arrows on her back, and hanging below them, a hatchet. Once she had everything ready she asked Storm to crawl onto the thick bed of moosehides on the travois. As they started out he noticed that the wolves kept a considerable distance from the horse. Every once in awhile the horse would snort when they got too close. Yet, the white wolf would occasionally come in close to the horse. Black would stretch his long neck down and touched muzzles with the wolf, as if they were reassuring one another that everything was all right. Storm shook his head in wonder.

They had gone about a mile into the trees when Rachel dismounted and walked back to Storm. He was startled and angry when she attempted to tie a bandana over his eyes. Storm pulled it away, glaring at her, and then grabbed her arm, pulling her off balance. Rachel landed on top of him. The nearness of him took her breath away. She deftly rolled on the ground scrambling to get away from him, but he jerked her back towards him. Holding her tight, he gently but firmly gathered her hair in his fingers and pulled her head towards him. When their lips met something alive and intense ran through Rachel's body. She felt as though she had become liquid and forgot all about struggling. Her whole body was in a state of shock as an unfamiliar burning desire took over her. What was happening to her? She was powerless over the urgent stirrings that were flooding her body.

What started in anger for Storm, who had only wanted to teach the wild one a lesson, changed in an instant. He had thought he was in control in this unexpected encounter, but he could not believe the intense emotions that overtook him. Never had he experienced such an overwhelming intensity as he was feeling with the woman-child in his arms. He'd had many women in his young life, but never one that had made him tremble with such uncontrollable passion. He had to fight off his instinct to control and dominate. Storm desperately wanted to become one with her. He held back.

Rachel, frightened and confused, yet drawn to this physical encounter, wrenched her head away from his and cried out in alarm. In a flash the white wolf flew at Storm, just as he released Rachel and rolled away. With powerful teeth snapping inches from his face, Storm held his breath, certain that he was going to lose his face again. He slowly picked up the blindfold, carefully reached over, and handed it to Rachel, who was frozen to the spot. She quietly spoke to Shadow, who gradually moved away from Storm's body, his lips still curled back and teeth flashing. Everything was quiet for a few moments, and then Rachel raised herself to her knees in a slow stupor, and gently placed the cloth over Storm's eyes, and tied it at the back of his head. Storm made no further attempt to remove the blindfold.

They travelled about four hours before stopping. Not a word was exchanged. Storm could hear running water as Rachel took the blindfold off and gave him food and drink. She told him, as she helped him to his feet, that she and the pack were going hunting. She quietly suggested that he walk around a bit and then try to get some rest. Leaving Wind as sentry, Rachel climbed up on Black and, along with the remaining five wolves, disappeared into the trees.

Storm wandered around aimlessly for a short time, then lied down and fell asleep. When he awakened he was hot and thirsty. He was so stiff and sore, he could only roll off the travois and crawl into the creek for a cooling drink. Wind didn't move. He just lay there watching the man, seemingly bored. But he didn't fool Storm one bit. He knew that if he made just one wrong move, the wolf would be on him. Besides, he had no intention of running away. Storm lay in the creek letting the cool water sooth his aching body, and wondering at its miraculous effect. Not only had the river cleansed his wounds. He was thoroughly convinced that the combination of the water and the girl's medicines had prevented a serious infection. Water had kept the raging fever at bay as well. He knew that if it hadn't been for Rachel's care he would surely be dead. Not many people would have survived the extent of injury he'd experienced. Still, he was surprised how long it was taking him to heal.

His mind wandered back to the kiss and the feel of Rachel's body, making him suck his breath in. What power she had over him. For the first time, it dawned on him that if she took him to his village it was not likely he would ever see her again. A gut-wrenching feeling arose in his stomach when he thought about this possibility.

A movement through the trees brought him back

to reality and he crawled out of the river to the moose-hide. Horse, rider, and the wolves appeared in a flurry of activity and excitement. Rachel had eleven prairie chickens flung over the horse. She dismounted, and he watched as she stepped on each chicken's feet and pulled on its neck until the meat slid out of the feathers and skin. Without wasting any time at all, she removed the innards and sliced off the heads, tossing them to the wolves. Rachel washed the chickens in the creek, carefully placed rocks around them, and left them there to cool. And then she gathered some kindling to start a fire.

In all this time, she didn't look Storm's way, intentionally avoiding his eyes. He slowly staggered to his feet. Wind, watching him stumbling around, walked over to him and stayed within reach. He seemed to be inviting Storm to lean on him for support. What was it that made the wolf help him? As far as he could see, Rachel hadn't signalled the wolf. Once Wind sensed that Storm wasn't going to fall, he simply baked off a little but continued to watch his movements.

Rachel was squatting down, cooking the chickens on a spit over the fire. Even without looking up she could tell that Storm was frustrated by his lack of strength and his incredibly weak muscles. By the time she looked up, he was standing in front of her.

"You must be patient," she said, "Your back was ripped open right down your spine." Rachel didn't know much about human anatomy and soft tissue, but her father had taught her quite a bit about the

structure of animals. She didn't have to be a doctor
to know that Storm' recovery was going to be slow.

If she hadn't insisted on getting him into the water
and forcing him to move his limbs, he may never have
walked again. She had no idea how far-reaching this
basic treatment could be. Initially, she had been doing
it simply to keep the wound clean, and she continued
only because she knew from her limited experience
that water feels good to a stiff and sore body.

Storm quietly sat down on the ground beside her
and she handed him some hot meat off the spit. He
bit into it with relish. There is nothing like fresh meat,
he thought. Rachel waited for him to say something
about the meal, hoping he might compliment her on
her hunting and cooking skills. But all he did when he
was done eating was give a huge belch and crawl on
his hands and knees back to the travois. "Ungrateful
heathen," she muttered to herself. Feeling confused
and a little hurt, she cleaned up the remains of the
meal and put things away. She spent the next few
minutes organizing things for morning. A few minutes later, she pulled out her sleeping hide, carefully
laid it by the fire, and quickly crawled in.

Storm, who had been watching her closely, was
surprised and asked why they weren't gong any further that day. Rachel told him she thought he'd had
enough and that they would try to go a little longer
tomorrow. Then she said, "Goodnight," and promptly
turned over. Hours later, Storm lay in the darkness
listening to her soft breathing, the rushing sound of
the flowing creek, and the quiet of the forest. The

65

moon cast a golden glow on everything it touched and the sky was brilliant with a dazzling display of stars. Perhaps it was a sign that this was a night for lovers, he mused. Then he caught himself and scoffed. Having kissed her against her will had ensured that she would keep her distance in the future. Why had he been so foolish, just when she was finally starting to trust him?

As Storm started to doze he realized that he'd always slept with one eye open, alert for danger, but since he'd been with Rachel he slept like the dead, knowing the wolves were protecting him. There he was, surrounded by savage animals, and he had never felt so safe in his entire life. With that bizarre thought he fell soundly into a deep sleep.

The next four days were similar to the first. They travelled for five or six hours, whatever Moon Beam felt Storm could endure. She knew where all the creeks were so Storm was able to get into the water every day to limber up and sooth his aching body. It soon became routine. While he was bathing and resting, Rachel would take the wolves and find something to eat, leaving Wind behind to guard the camp.

On this particular day, they had stopped in the early afternoon for a meal and a lengthy rest. Storm was glad for a break from the travois and was lying luxuriously on a hide watching Rachel 's every move. Although he would never have admitted it, was grudgingly impressed by this woman-child. He wondered how she was able to supply food every night without fail. Many times Storm felt something stirring in his heart for her as she moved around the campsite. When he saw her struggling with a task that was obviously too much for her he frequently found himself wanting to help her. He didn't understand this feeling at all as he had never experienced anything like it. One thing was certain. He had never been in love and was just as unfamiliar with these puzzling emotions as Rachel was, even if he was eight years older than her. He was thankful he now had clothes to cover him, not so much to protect him from the elements but to hide his manhood. He'd discovered in the last few days that his body was reacting to her more frequently. And the more his body betrayed him the more intrigued he became with her. He couldn't believe another being, especially a woman, could make him feel so out of control. And even more unbelievable — a white woman.

The wolves were out doing whatever it is that wolves do and Rachel was finalizing preparations to move on again. She stood at the edge of the clearing for a while as though she were listening for something. A few wolves quietly appeared at her side. She sent two or three of them ahead as scouts, and then very slowly and cautiously followed after them. Only Wind and Black remained behind with Storm. Several minutes later, and well out of sight of the camp, she stopped again to listen. She didn't want to be seen or heard, nor did she want to endanger her wolves. As they cautiously made their way across a creek she suddenly heard what she thought were human screams, at least they sounded human. In a few moments the wolves were close around her, clearly agitated. Rachel moved toward the screams, picked up her pace a little, and motioned the wolves to follow. They knew not to take their eyes off her. The hunt was on. All vocal sounds within the group stopped and Rachel switched to hand signals. Storm had heard the screams too, and was highly alarmed.

As the wolves and Rachel slowly got closer, she looked down over the bank of a creek and saw a deeply disturbing scene less than fifty yards from her. Her wolves immediately hunched down beside her flat to the ground.

CHAPTER 7

A Dramatic Rescue

There were four men and they had three captive Indian women with them. One of the men was struggling to hold a woman down while another was brutally savaging her. The other two men were trying the force the two remaining women to the ground, brutally beating them into submission. Rachel's stomach filled with bile. She had never seen the sex act between humans but she knew it wasn't supposed to be like this. Something was terribly wrong here. These men were committing an unspeakable act. She firmly motioned the wolves to stay where they were, and ran back to get Black. On her way she met Storm who was painfully making his way through the trees towards the commotion. Wind was beside him. She frantically motioned for him to stay down and maintain silence as she ran past him headed for the horse.

Grabbing Black's mane she swung up onto his back. The horse, sensing her urgency, was instantly on the run. They thundered past Storm who had almost made it to the creek bank. The wolves caught sight of Rachel and waited, poised for action. She signalled the wolves to surround the men, and then pulling out an arrow she fastened it to the shaft of her bow. As she squeezed her knees tight the horse broke into a gallop. Storm reached the top of the bank just as the horse raced past him towards the creek at full gallop. Rachel knew that there was a four-to-five-foot drop down into the creek bed, and just as they reached the bank of the creek Black saw the open space. Rachel abruptly pulled back on the reins, Black raised his head, and they were airborne. She let go of the reins just before they landed, and as they came down she whistled to signal the wolves to attack.

The mighty creatures were on the men in seconds. Rachel let her arrow fly and hit the man who was still restraining the woman he'd ravaged. One dead, she thought, as Shadow hit another of the attackers who was sprawled over one of the other two women. At the same time, Bolt and Wind had the one who had been slapping and wrestling the woman who was not yet down. The fourth man stood up and ran for his gun. Just before he got to it Rachel swung Black around and threw her hatchet, hitting him in the back of his head. As he went down Cloud and Salt were right on top of him. Rachel grabbed for the knife on her waist, grasping it tightly in her hand as she jumped off Black, and headed towards Shadow who was mauling his prey. The man was on his knees trying to get up when she plunged the knife into his back and left Shadow to finish him off.

Storm, who had watched the attack in horror from the top of the bank, couldn't believe that four men were dead on the ground. Not one of them had had a moment to fight for his life. What a warrior this young girl was! Where had she learned to shoot a bow from the back of a running horse? Throwing that hatchet was no accident. He laboriously made his way down the bank to the women. As he picked his way down, several small children, who had been hiding in the bush appeared, terrified and crying. He stopped to comfort them and told them everything was going to be all right.

Rachel, in the meantime, turned her attention to her wolves calling them to her. The man who had the hatchet in him was still struggling, so Rachel calmly walked over to him and slit his throat. His eyes widened in death and at the same time Rachel recognized him as the man that had attacked her mother years ago. "You were right Daddy, he was no good," she said.

Rachel turned to the man Wind and Bolt had taken down. They had done their work well, his throat had been chewed out and his blood was pouring onto the ground. Black was blowing and pawing the ground as Rachel walked over to calm him. She finally noticed the children, who were by this time running to their mothers. One of the women started screaming again and Rachel looked back to see what was wrong. She spotted a small figure laying face down in the water and ran for the creek. Picking the baby up, she immediately started to breathe into its tiny mouth. Storm was beside her now, and as she placed the infant in his arms he instinctively took over and laid the child on the ground. Rachel was completely out of breath and couldn't continue the resuscitation. But Storm took over, alternating gentle breaths with pressure on her diaphragm. By this time, Rachel was sobbing, and as he worked on the baby Storm could hear her pleading softly, "Please don't die ... please don't die."

Suddenly the little one took a breath, gagged, and started to throw up. Storm turned her gently on her side and another ragged breath emerged from her tiny body. He sat cross-legged holding her gently as tears fell from his eyes. The girl child in his arms was his sister's baby.

The three women were hysterical and afraid of the wolves that were still snarling and mauling at the men. Rachel whistled and the barking and snarling ceased. The wolves backed away from their kills and instantly lay down watching for Rachel's next move. Storm called to the women and they ran to him, then to each other, sobbing and talking in their own language. One of them came and took the little girl from Storm's arms. Sobbing and blinded by tears she couldn't believe the child was breathing. Just a few moments ago she had watched in despair as one of the men had callously tossed her baby into the water. She had fought desperately to get away and to save her baby.

As Rachel watched the mothers holding and hugging their children tightly, a lump formed in her throat. She remembered her own mother's hugs and kisses when she had been hurt or afraid. It had been along time since she had felt a loved one's gentle touch. In that moment she decided to leave Storm there with his people. One of the women could go to the village for help and this would give her time to disappear with Black and the wolves.

Rachel wiped the blood from her knife on the grass and returned it to its sheath. Then she walked over to the man with the hatchet in his head and pulled it out, cleaned it, and placed it around her neck. Then, exhausted, she weakly whistled to the wolves and dragged herself up onto Black.

As she disappeared into the trees, she looked back at Storm, who was comforting his sister, the other two women, and the children. He hadn't noticed her departure. A lump formed in Rachel's throat and a great sense of sadness and loss overtook her. As she headed for the campsite and the empty travois she began to cry. She couldn't understand her own tears. After all, he was nothing more than a menace to her and her wolves. Sick and heartbroken over what she had witnessed, she vowed that she would always pro-tect her family, the wolves and her horse, at any cost.

CHAPTER 8

A Long Lonely Winter

When Storm turned around to look for Rachel he couldn't believe she was gone. He called her name several times but it was like the forest had swallowed the woman-child and her constant companions. There wasn't a sound or the whisper of a breeze. Everything that had just happened seemed unreal. Maybe she was a spirit. One moment she was there taking care of them all, and in the next she vanished. The days he had spent with her and the wolves ... the things he had seen ... the connection between her and her wolves. Maybe it was all a dream.

Storm felt disappointment and despair. Then, gradually, his feelings turned to anger. The waif did whatever she wanted without any thought for his feelings. How dare she ride away without saying goodbye? She hadn't given him a chance to take her to his people. He had wanted to tell her that she would have safe passage to his village whenever she wanted it, and that she would never again have to steal food.

The tribe could have become a safe haven for her and her wolves. Her stubborn independence had denied him all this. Storm pounded on the ground where he was sitting.

"Take me home," he said to his small group. As they travelled the last few miles to their village Storm told them of his encounter with the grizzly, and of how the girl had sewed him back together. He told them how she put him in the river to keep his fever down, and that she had made him walk in the river to make his legs work. Storm tried to explain her strange relationship with the land and the wolves. He was hurting. And it wasn't his physical injuries.

Once they we back at their village, the women lifted his shirt to look at his back and were horrified at the extent of his wounds. They were still a shocking mess but the wounds were healing, and there were no signs of infection. As Storm explained in great detail about how to keep the wounds clean and about the disgusting tea mould Rachel made him drink, both he and the women began to think that maybe they had a new way to save lives when their own people suffered wounds and infectious diseases.

As summer moved into fall, Storm was still haunted by the experience. His chest felt so heavy he some-times thought he was going to suffocate. At those times his rage against her would rise and consume him. How could she have left him like that? But even in his fury, he knew she cared about him. There was nothing he could do. He couldn't search for her, as he was still far too weak. He knew he had to wait until his body healed. So he started to push himself, spending hours in the river, moving his legs, walking and bending, forcing his body to do as much as it possibly could. The pain continued, but now it was mostly in his heart.

By the time the November winds came and winter was upon them, Storm was back on his horse and walking with ease. The open sores on his back, which Rachel hadn't been able to sew shut, formed permanent scars as they healed over with new flesh. He had been sick and weak for a very long time and the trauma was now behind him. However, he was obsessed by thoughts of Rachel.

In January, Storm took a hunting party and headed towards the area where he believed Rachel lived, hoping to find some sign of her or the wolves. They saw wolf tracks and horse signs but never the girl. They hunted for two weeks before they gave up and headed for home. The men avoided talking to him because of his sour mood. Fast Creek was the only one who had the nerve to break the silence. "Your heart aches for that woman," he said to Storm, suddenly breaking a long silence. Their proud chief had been unreasonable all day. Storm gulped, was that what was wrong with him? That was not possible, he was a proud and noble chief, his people depended on him. He had no need for a woman and no time for frivolous matters of the heart.

Nevertheless, he vowed to himself that in the spring he would follow the river until he found the place where he had laid helplessly on the ground.

He'd had nothing else to do through two full moons but to look at every tree and rock around that riverbank, if he could just find that clearing he was sure he'd be able to find Rachel 's dwelling.

Meanwhile, the winter passed slowly for Rachel. Although she was fully occupied hunting for food and training the young wolves, she was lonely. She couldn't understand this as she had been alone for years and had grown used to solitude. After all, she had Black and her family of wolves. She wondered what was wrong with her and why she was feeling so restless?

Storm was on her mind a lot and sometimes she let her thoughts wander. What would it be like to make love with a man? She always became extremely unsettled when she relived their embrace, and she was strangely fascinated yet uncomfortable with her feelings. But she tried to push the memory from her mind. Having Storm around had awakened the need in her for human contact, but it was more than that. She recalled watching Shadow and Honey romp around showing their affection for each other and she remembered how her mother and father used to snuggle together or hold each other tight for comfort. As she reminisced about these things she began to realize what the problem was. Her mother had talked to her about love and why men and women needed each other. She had explained the kinds of love people experience. Could it be that she had fallen in love with Storm? No. That wasn't possible. Not that sullen and arrogant Indian! But then again her mother had told her many fairy tales and love stories, and she had also told her how there seemed to be no rhyme or reason why people fell in love.

But how she could she ever love Storm? She was sure it wasn't even possible. He had been surly and rude, and he never thanked her for anything she did for him. He'd made taking care of him an ordeal. He had never looked at or talked to her without frowning or sulking. Even the wolves reacted to his disposition. But of course, you could hardly blame him. What did he know about wolves? They were just something to hunt and to kill for their fur. He seemed to think they didn't have feelings. She'd had to explain to him that if one of them were killed the whole packed mourned, that they actually felt grief and sorrow. It was a good thing he had been so weak or he would never have allowed her to help him at all. What was the sense of thinking that their worlds could ever come together?

Spring finally arrived and the ice on the river began to break up. The river thundered and screeched as enormous chunks of ice broke and were dramatically shoved up onto the shore. Rachel remembered her father telling her that when the river ice broke up it was the month of April. Day by day more game appeared, signalling that hunting would soon get easier for her and the pack. Black's mares were foaling so Rachel kept the wolf pack well away from the herd, as the wolves made the high-strung stallion even more nervous when they came near his mares.

Ebony had a litter of pups and, to Rachel 's delight, a pure white one immerged, the same colour as its father. And then, a little male pup that was as black as a piece of coal came right after. She named the female Snow and, of course, the male pup was named Coal. The other two were grey in colour so she called them Pepper and Cloud.

The pack began to break up when some of the males refused to submit to Shadow's leadership. If they lost a fight with Shadow, and they always did, they had no choice but to leave the pack. Once banned from the pack, some of the stronger males would manage to take a few females with them. Shadow fought hard to stay at the top and Rachel knew it would take a very big and bold male to take him down. Still, she could see that the fighting took its toll on him. But such was the call of the wild. Rachel never mixed in, no matter how sorry she felt for the giant wolf. But no matter how many of them Shadow banned, they remained her friends and occasionally snuck back to the cabin to visit her. Or when she was out walking alone they would find her, always making sure that Shadow wasn't around. If they decided to rejoin the pack they had to show their submission to Shadow by lying on their backs, and also by never raising their tails in his presence. Only the dominant reigning male did this. It was a sometimes-puzzling pecking order, but it seemed to work in the overall scheme of things.

One day, when Ebony's pups were about six weeks old, Rachel and the pack decided to go hunting. As Rachel walked she wondered about Storm. She had spotted him and his band at the beginning of winter when they were searching for her. She had kept hidden for a few days, making sure to light only wood she knew would not smoke. Then she had followed them for a few days, amused by hunting the hunters. Rachel was so close to them she thought about sending the wolf pack into their midst during the night. They didn't seem to know much about wolves. She was surprised that they assumed they could sneak up on her. Instead, Rachel returned to her cabin and made sure the wolves lay low for a while. She was pretty sure they were safe because Storm and his band had been hunting for them in all the wrong places.

CHAPTER 9

Return of the Grizzly

As the hunt for food proceeded Rachel noticed the wolves seemed unusually jumpy that day. They were about four miles from the cabin when she began noticing grizzly markings on the trees. Just as she gave the signal for the pack to move out of the area the grizzly attacked. She was sure it was the crazed one, because if a grizzly were merely hunting, it would know there were wolves around, and would leave the area to avoid danger. She'd had a feeling the grizzly was stalking them, and her instinct was confirmed when he suddenly came up behind them.

Rachel, who was on foot, ran to a tree as soon as she caught sight of the bear. As she frantically climbed as high as she could she heard the snarling and fighting below her. Helplessly, she watched as her wolves went after the bear. She whistled the command get away from the beast, but for some reason Ebony lunged at the bear instead. Reaching out with its powerful claws, the grizzly caught her in mid-air

81

and swiped at the side of her head. Rachel heard the snap as Ebony's neck broke.

At that point, she gave the command to attack and the wolves flew at the bear with a vengeance. The enraged grizzly killed two more wolves before giving ground and lumbering off into the bush with the pack in close pursuit. When Rachel lost sight of the bear she scrambled down the tree and ran to Ebony. Holding her wolf in her arms she rocked back and forth, crying a flood of tears, but she knew there was nothing she could do for this gentle wolf that had been her friend for the last seven years.

That's the way Shadow found them when he and the pack returned. Bathed in Ebony's blood Rachel reached out to Shadow who lied down beside her, and put his big paws on top of his mate. Whining, he tried to wake her up. Rachel let go of Ebony and moved away to let Shadow sniff at her and try to rouse her. She knew there was no sense trying to move her until Shadow realized that there was no life left in his companion. Shadow was beside himself. Although he killed regularly and always recognized and accepted death, he seemed to be in denial as he licked at the blood on his mate's face and continued to paw at her. He grabbed her coat of fur with his teeth and tried to drag her around in an effort to make her get up.

At the same time Rachel had begun to dig a grave with her hatchet. It was a long process because she had to bury three wolves. When she was done she rested and waited until Shadow had exhausted himself. There was no use continuing until the wolf had accepted that his mate was dead because Rachel knew he would fight her off. Finally, the wolf gave up and lay down with his head on top of Ebony. Rachel got up and went to him holding his big head in her hands. "Can I take her now Shadow?" she asked.

Pulling Ebony and the other two wolves into the grave wasn't easy, as they each weighed around one hundred pounds. And Shadow wasn't about to help with this one. Once the hole was covered Rachel whistled for the rest of the pack and headed for home with them, leaving Shadow lying beside his mate's grave. Rachel cried all the way to the cabin. She had a big job ahead of her. Ebony's pups were at home waiting for their mother. Rachel knew she was going to have a hard time saving the litter. But she soon stiffened her back and went to work. She'd saved a litter once before and she could do it again. Shadow stayed at the grave for four days going without food and water. On the fifth day he announced his arrival back home by scratching at the cabin door.

Rachel opened the door and he walked in and went straight to the cubs to regurgitate the contents of his stomach. As Shadow's meal was already partly digested the hungry pups had no trouble eating the soft offering. Now this would be their only food as there was no way of providing milk for them. Shadow now had to take on Ebony's job of feeding the pups.

The pups were reassured and happy and rolled on the floor beneath him. Shadow was so tall that the only way he could play with the tiny pups was to lie down. When he was standing they didn't even reach the top of his legs, but when he was down on the floor they immediately started wrestling and biting on his huge feet. Later, Shadow watched as the pups continued to play, jumping and racing around the cabin until they knocked over the water bucket, spilling water across the floor.

Rachel didn't have the heart to stop the playful interaction. The pups had missed their mother and the milk she supplied, and Rachel had only been able to give them warm water and small pieces of meat. Shadow finally settled down and let the pups crawl all over his big body. They could now bite his muzzle. One puppy had Shadow's ear in his mouth and was tugging it back and forth. Another had made it to the top of his father's head and was snarling and growling as if he were attacking a real enemy. Rachel sat by the fire, laughing at their antics. Contentment settled around the cabin as the healing process began. She was devastated by the loss of Ebony. Besides Shadow, Ebony was the wolf that had spent the most time with her. This was because Rachel was usually the substitute den mother to the litter of pups born each year. This time it was different. Shadow sensed that he was now solely responsible for the pups, and pushed them extra hard as he taught them how to survive in the pack.

Fawn became Shadow's new mate. She had a quiet nature and was relatively small, and Shadow dwarfed Fawn. Rachel wondered why he'd picked such a small animal to be the dominant female of the pack. She knew there would be times Fawn would have to fight when bigger females went into heat and challenged her position.

After Ebony's death, Rachel threw herself into the training of the pups and the summer flew by. Soon it was August. Almost a year had gone by since her time with Storm and she often thought about him. It seemed strange that they had not crossed paths in their travels. But then again, she had kept a low profile with the pups and had gone hunting only when necessary. The wolves were always nearby, coming or going, and it seemed to her that they were enjoying their leisurely summer as much as she was. Outside of putting up firewood and finding food to dry for the winter Rachel had a peaceful and relaxing summer.

CHAPTER 10

A Fortuitous Find and a Deadly Encounter

One afternoon Rachel was wading in the river with the pups when one of them came to her with something in his mouth. She could see it was a gold-colour and had come from the water. She explored further, wading around the shallow edge of the river, fascinated by the multitude of nuggets she found lying in the shallow water. Rachel gathered them for days, hauling them home and hiding them in the secret storage room. She had no idea what she was going to use them for but they might come in handy for something someday. They were gold nuggets and must have washed down from the hills into the creek that ran into the river. Although Rachel didn't know it at the time, she had suddenly become very wealthy.

Meanwhile, Storm and his braves hunted regularly to get enough food to carry their people through the winter. Aside from this he didn't do much else — except search for Rachel. His people didn't move from place to place as some tribes did. This was their territory and every other tribe respected that. He was feeling quite strong by this time. The slight limp that remained in one leg was only noticeable when he was tired. The women still talked about the white-haired girl, who had come galloping in on a big black horse surrounded by wolves to save them. With every telling the story got more and more impressive. The women were convinced that the woman-child was an elusive she-spirit who looked after them and their village. They left extra food and grain out for her now that it was fall.

When Storm tried to explain that she was flesh and blood and lived with the wolves they would just raise their eyebrows at him. They knew better. All you had to do was look at his back and face to know that only a spirit with awesome powers could have healed such wounds. Also, the white-haired one could control wolves. She couldn't possibly be from this world. Finally, Storm gave up trying to convince them. He would have to find her and bring her back to his tribe before they would believe him. He had heard their whispers, people saying they thought he was fine and that his head had healed well since his ordeal. He seemed okay they said, until the waif was mentioned. Then he would try to tell them that she was real. But they concluded that their great chief was, sadly, in love with a spirit.

Storm became more determined than ever to find Rachel. Sometimes he followed the river for miles, and occasionally he spotted the wolves. But every time he got close, they disappeared. Only once did he spot the white wolf but it vanished like a puff of smoke. A few times during the year he had seen tracks and other signs near the village and wondered if she was nearby. Once in a while, he got the strongest feeling that she was watching him. Why couldn't he find her, or even catch a glimpse of her?

It had been raining for a week. Rachel had stayed near the cabin and hadn't seen much of the wolves. She knew they had dens here and there and that they were waiting out the rain. Rachel checked the stew in the pot. It needed more water. She walked over to the water bucket only to find it was almost empty. She would have to go down to the river to replenish her water supply. Rachel carefully put on her cloak with the hood. She liked it because it kept her warm and dry, but more than that, when she had it on she felt as though she were invisible. She walked out toward the riverbank, almost half-a-mile down a gradual slope. The trail wound through the thick trees to the steep riverbank. She had used this trail so many times that she could find her way in the dark.

The rain was coming down in torrents as she started down the bank. She was almost into the clearing when the grizzly appeared. He came out of nowhere. Rachel had heard nothing and had seen no signs of the bear. With no wolves beside her to give a warning she had walked right into the bear. Or had it found her intentionally?

The bear came straight at her, forcing her to the edge of the steep bank. Rachel gave a frightened whistle just before the saturated ground let go under her feet. Suddenly, she plunged down, landing in a hollow with part of the cliff on top of her. Everything went black and still. Was it the fall that rendered her unconscious or was it the snapping of her leg? When she came to, the wolves were yelping from up top and making attempts to climb down to her. Rachel knew she was in big trouble. She couldn't move at all, as a huge hill of dirt and debris were pinning her down. Even if she could get free there was no way she could climb to the top of the bank. Excruciating pain confirmed that she had broken her leg. Crying out, she called, "Shadow!" Shadow, "Go get Black."

She wasn't sure what good the horse could do but she knew she'd be safer if he was with her. And she knew the bear must be nearby. Rachel tried pulling and wiggling to get out from beneath the bank of dirt. She was digging with her fingers to scrape the mud away when Black appeared at the top, whinnying to her. "Black, take Shadow. Go get Storm." She could hear the wolves whining above and around her, and she knew she was about to pass out again. "I ... need ... help," she weakly told the animals.

Some of the wolves had slowly made their way down the mudslide to her. As animals tend to do when they are frightened, they had kept her in sight and called to her over the bank instead of trying to follow the trail. Rachel kept drifting in and out of consciousness. At one point she heard a terrible commotion. The grizzly had returned. If the wolves couldn't drive the bear away he would soon kill her. It seemed forever before the snarling and roaring stopped. Rachel was gasping for air. Not only was her leg broken, but also the mounting debris was slowly crushing her. As she slipped into a semi-conscious state she could feel the wolves trying to dig her out, but the dirt was heavy rock-laden mud. Eventually Bolt came and lay down beside her, exhausted. He licked her face, as if telling her he didn't know what to do next.

Suddenly, he got up and started to howl. The other wolves joined in howling non-stop. Rachel had never heard the wolves howl quite like that. Maybe they knew she was going to die. Animals have an uncanny sense when it comes to these things, she thought. She feebly tried to free her arms but her hands were numb and no longer able to function. Finally, weak from exhaustion, the world around her ceased to exist.

In the meantime, Black and Shadow were pounding through the trees. Every once in a while the big wolf would stop and howl as the horse thundered on. They were the most mournful howls he had ever heard. Each time Shadow howled something deep inside the horse told him that the big white wolf was crying.

They reached the Indian village at daybreak causing considerable commotion. The huge white wolf at the tree line howling in a terrifying way had abruptly awakened everyone. Most of Storm's people thought something supernatural was happening. The big black stallion was running in and out of the village and no one could get near him. Each time he galloped through he pounded back to the wolf and stood there, as though he were watching for someone he knew. What on earth was happening? Were they being attacked by enemies or by evil spirits?

Storm raced through the camp just in time to catch sight of the two frenzied animals. Shadow came in closer when he saw Storm running towards him, then he stopped dead in his tracks, only a few feet from Storm, and let out a desperate howl. Then the wolf ran back to Black and turned to look at Storm, urging him to follow. When Storm attempted to run back to the camp to get his horse and weapons the wolf ran at him. Grabbing Storm by his sleeve and clenching his teeth firmly but carefully on Storm's forearm he gave the man no alternative but to follow him. Storm already knew in his heart something had happened to Rachel. He hollered at his braves, telling them to get the horses and follow Black and the wolf.

By now Storm was running freely with Shadow but every time his pace slacked off the wolf would burst ahead and then turn back to grab Storm's arm again. It was clear to anyone watching that the wolf's powerful jaws could have broken Storm's arm in an instant. As Storm got close to Black, the horse edged closer to him, urging him to get on his back. Storm hadn't realized just how tall Black was until he swung himself up on the great beast's back. It must have been nearly impossible for that little wisp of a thing to swing herself up onto the horse, but he had seen her do it many times.

As Black turned and started to run with him on his back, Storm could feel the surge of the horse's muscles as they flexed under his body. Black was sweating profusely as he had already run a long way, but the urgency he displayed showed that he was prepared to run just as hard back to where he had come from. Storm was beginning to feel a deep dread inside. What was wrong? What had happened to Rachel? She was either very badly injured or dead; because there was no way that these two animals would ever leave her side if she were merely in danger. Not only that, the two had entered the village in broad daylight, something they would never do under normal circumstances. Storm let the horse find his own pace and the wolf ran alongside.

Black's pace was fast for ten or fifteen minutes, then for one or two miles he'd slow to a fast trot. Once his laboured breathing eased off he'd break into a gallop to catch up with the wolf. The wolf seldom varied his pace. When the horse slowed down he just kept running because he knew that once Black started his run he would catch up to him.

Storm figured it might be a long way to Rachel, and that the horse must have already run that distance to get his help. A lump formed in Storm's throat when he thought about this gallant horse and the devoted wolf running beside him. And, for the first time, Storm realized the extent of his feelings for her. He had never been afraid of anyone or anything but he was beginning to realize that this feeling of dread, this unfamiliar knot in his stomach, was fear. Oddly, the full realization of his love for her and the sudden fear that she might be taken away from him were equally painful. These unfamiliar feelings were disturbing, but he knew one thing for sure. If she were dead he would never feel whole again. In that moment, the urgency of the wolf and the horse convinced him that she was still alive. He had to get to her before it was too late. He had to look after her.

They had started out in the early morning and it was now getting dark. The horse had been running all night and now all day with a rider on his back so Storm was convinced they would make it back to Rachel by dawn, that is, if they weren't killed in the dark. The moonlight would help somewhat but Storm was worried the dark would slow them down.

As the night set in Storm felt the horse's muscles starting to bunch under him and he instinctively tightened his knees to the animal's sides as they left the ground. Having already landed on the other side of a four-foot chasm the wolf was waiting for them. Storm sensed that the wolf was guiding Black in the dark and alerting the horse to the dangers in front of them. He had no idea how the wolf and the horse were communicating with each other, but knew they must be.

Storm hoped his braves were on the alert for the ravine because if they weren't some of them would get badly hurt. He could sense Black's impending exhaustion. The animal wasn't running full out anymore, or as far, before breaking into a trot, but Storm did nothing to hurry him. The horse had to go his own pace or he would not make it. He wasn't a young horse anymore and this could very well be his last run.

Storm knew they had arrived at their destination when they started down an abrupt and disturbed embankment. As they neared the bottom they were enthusiastically greeted by the wolves, who seemed to be everywhere, howling and barking as they all mingled together. He lost no time in jumping off Black's back when they reached the wolves. In the semi-darkness he could see a mound of bank that had obviously given way. As his eyes frantically searched the pile of debris he saw a pale hand.

He ran towards Rachel stumbling over rocks and sliding in the mud. He was terrified he wouldn't be able to get her out of there before the rest of the bank gave way. They had disturbed the unstable ground even more on their descent and it could go at any moment. Rachel had been under that mound for a long time and was barley breathing. He was amazed she was still alive. He talked to her as he dug but there was no response. She was in a world of her own.

At first Storm was relieved when he saw his braves making their way down the bank, until he realized they were likely making it even more unstable. He had made little progress in the mud. How had his men, who had fallen far behind Black and Shadow, found them? Fast Creek told him that one of the wolves had stayed behind to guide them and had led them straight to the collapsed bank. The braves worked together pushing felled trees just above the mound to prevent the mud from caving in on the woman-child as they dug. After considerable effort they finally managed to dig Rachel free from her makeshift grave. Her cloak was saturated with mud and water, but being moosehide it had protected her and kept her fairly warm. They had to strip it from her because its cumbersome weight made it difficult to lift her. Once Storm had her up in his arms he knew he had to find shelter immediately. She was not at all responsive and he feared the worst. Just then Shadow mouthed his thigh to get his attention and Black instinctively moved in beside him.

Never had Storm or his braves experienced anything like what came next. Black lay down with his legs under him, and then Storm stepped over his back and onto the horse with the girl still in his arms. Horses, braves, and wolves then cautiously started up the bank following Storm and the girl. Once on top of the hill it was obvious the wolf and horse were headed somewhere specific, and Storm knew in his heart it was Rachel's dwelling.

CHAPTER 11

The Great Wolf's Recovery

It was a cloudy and foggy dawn. When the wolf and the horse stopped only a few minutes after they started out, Storm didn't understand what they were doing. He couldn't see a dwelling or shelter of any kind, but climbed off the horse, still holding Rachel. It was clear that Black wasn't going any further. Just then Shadow barked for the Indian to follow. Storm followed the wolf behind a thicket of dense trees and shrubs and was taken aback to see a wooden structure with two shuttered tight windows and a door with a heavy bar across it. Still holding the girl, he motioned for one of his men to open the door. It was still dark inside.

One of Storm's men set about igniting the torch he carried. Meanwhile, Storm cautiously entered and gently laid Rachel on a bed. Within minutes the braves had a made a fire in the fireplace. Storm told the men he needed more light so he could look her over. He knew her leg was broken and she had a terrible bruise on the side of her face. He would have to wash her body first as he couldn't tell the extent of her injuries with all the mud and debris on her. The braves quickly cut a deerhide in pieces and wrapped them tightly around a sturdy stick. After dunking it in the bucket of bear fat beside the stove they held it over the fire until it caught, then carefully placed it into the torch holder close to the bed.

On a signal from their chief they left the cabin so that Storm could remove Rachel's damp clothes. He carefully removed or cut what clothing he could, washed her body, and covered her with a large soft hide. Then he called Fast Creek to come and help him with Rachel's leg. Storm was glad that she was still unconscious because what they had to do to set her leg was going to be horrible. When the two men were done Fast Creek left and Storm checked her from head to toe, looking for additional injuries. He noticed a sizeable lump and a swelling on her head that ran down the side of her face to the dark bruise. That's why she was out cold. She must have taken a severe blow on the head and Storm knew that was not a good sign. He'd seen people in comas before. He'd once had a friend who remained that way for two weeks and then died. Storm felt a sickening dread wash over him. Maybe, hidden by the swelling, her skull was crushed.

The next morning one of the braves opened the door and asked Storm to come out. As Storm stepped out into the morning sunlight he couldn't believe his eyes. All around the cabin and on top of the cabin, which was built into the earth on a hillside, were wolves. There were dozens of them. Storm felt the hair on his neck stand up and goose bumps rise on his arms. The ponies were very skittish, snorting and puffing and working themselves into a lather. If they hadn't been securely tied they'd have been long gone.

It was a most unusual sight. In the midst of all those wolves stood the big black horse with the white wolf by his side. Black was very agitated. Storm quietly picked handfuls of long grass and slowly approached the animal. He talked soothingly while he rubbed the horse down. Storm was awed and comforted by Black's complete acceptance of him. As he worked on the horse he looked around. The wolves were from different packs, each with their own dominant males and females. It was obvious that several were Shadow's offspring. Storm marvelled at how the wolves knew something was wrong with Rachel and how they communicated in order to gather together. Apparently Bolt's sporadic howling throughout the night was not only grief but also a summons for council. After all, the girl was their alpha wolf and she was in trouble.

The horse knew how they had come to be there. From the moment the core group had headed toward the Indian village, the giant white wolf had put out the distress call. The wolves had travelled from all directions and were still appearing. And the horse, now surrounded by these powerful animals, stood alone. The only wolf that dared to venture close to him was Shadow. Storm had never seen this kind of behaviour before. If another wolf came too close the horse would try to tramp on it while Shadow lunged at the intruder to chase it back to its clan. It was a tense situation, but there was respect and an order to things that only the horse and the wolves understood. They kept their distance, but nothing could move them away from their established positions around the cabin.

On the second day Rachel became semi-conscious, moving ever so slightly, only to fade back into herself, someplace deep inside her body where she felt safe. Storm's heart sank as he pleaded with her to stay in this world. Day faded into night as Storm stayed by the side of the bed watching her. She was beautiful lying there with her long white hair framing her face. He wondered how he could possibly describe her. She would have to have an Indian name. As the moonlight from the full moon filtered through the cabin windows and fell on her face, he suddenly realized that his White spirit waif had just been given a new name. And from that moment on she became Moon Beam to Storm.

At about noon on the third day, Moon Beam regained consciousness. She was vulnerable and shy as Storm gently lifted her head to give her a drink of water. Several hours later he fed her a little soup and helped her to the edge of the bed. He then held her up so she could relieve herself in a container that he'd found under the bed. As Storm lifted her back into the bed she gave a weak whistle, and in bounded Shadow. The huge wolf howled a greeting and then gently put his paws on the bed and licked her face.

The tears fell softly as she started to cry, and the last thought she had before she went back to sleep was that her wolf had saved her life.

The next day, in the grey dawn of morning, she awoke and lay there watching Storm as he slept on her old bed. He looked exhausted, but peaceful. Her hands were hurting and she examined them closely. She was alarmed to discover that her nails were broken and torn to the quick, and her fingers and hands were covered with oozing wounds. Although she didn't remember much about her ordeal she clearly recalled clawing desperately at the muddy mass. She didn't know that Storm had put her hands in salt water and let them soak for hours as she slept. She was trying to figure everything out. How had Storm got her out and how had he found her cabin? Probably Shadow, she surmised, he likes Storm. She hoped her wolves were keeping out of sight because she had seen other braves coming and going and they were just as foreboding as Storm was. She wondered if they ever laughed or smiled.

On the fifth day Storm told his braves to return to the village, as he knew their people would be worried and wondering what had happened to them. He told the men to tell everyone that the waif was not a phantom, that she was a real human being and had almost died. The only thing different about her was that she was White and she lived with wolves and a big black horse. That should go down really well and stir things up again as to her origins. "One more thing," Storm said, "Tell them Storm is not as crazy as they think." Some of his braves dropped their heads, and Storm could tell they had frequently discussed his mental state amongst themselves. Now they were headed for home to tell what they had seen, and they knew everyone was going to think they'd all been smoking something.

Storm was gentle with Moon Beam and very quiet. Little by little he told her how Shadow and Black had come to the village for him. No, her wolves hadn't stayed out of sight. They were all over the place, even worrying him when he went to get water. They would disappear to hunt for a few hours but then return as soon as possible, as there were very young wolf pups among the different packs. Apparently they had not been left behind. Every one of them came. One could easily differentiate between the packs. The alpha wolves, both male and female, kept their tails high and more or less kept to themselves. There were seven packs in all, and the only time the dominant males of a pack dropped their tails was when Shadow walked in close. There was no doubt about it, the other pack leaders always submitted to the great white wolf. Storm knew that he would never witness anything like this again in his lifetime. He was in awe over how these wild animals cared so much about this unusual woman. Wolves had never crossed his mind much, as he had only thought of them as fur pelts. He had never thought about the possibility of them being loyal to a human being. Storm was certainly getting a lesson on wolf behaviour.

On the eighth day, Storm packed Moon Beam

outside and sat her on the bench in front of the cabin. When she saw all the packs she started to laugh. Storm hadn't been kidding when he told her there were a great number of wolves. When he heard her laughter he threw his head back and laughed with her. Rachel's breath caught. He really could laugh. What a wonderful sound it was. A few minutes later, he told her the spirits had named her Moon Beam. She didn't know what to think at first. But then, after saying it a few times in her head, she decided she liked it. Besides, at that moment in the warm sun, she did feel she'd been reborn and believed it was entirely possible that spirits had been responsible.

Slowly, in small groups, the wolves that were familiar with Moonbeam came to greet her. The others, offspring of the wolves that had left Shadow's pack, stayed back and watched. They came in all sizes and colours. Yipping and howling, they seemed to be celebrating her recovery. What astounded Storm was that Shadow stayed back watching it all and let the others welcome her. This great white wolf was actually sharing Moon Beam, and he seemed to sense that she belonged to all of them. Storm came to a startling conclusion as he watched her with the wolves. They didn't consider her a human being. To them she was the leader of all the wolves — she was The Great Wolf.

Moon Beam went back to sleep after spending two hours with her wolves, and slept straight through until morning. Storm suspected there was something seriously wrong with her by this time because she wasn't healing as quickly as he'd anticipated. He had to get her back to his village so the women could look after her. Healing was their domain and he had very little knowledge of their healing plants and herbs. The next day Storm told Moon Beam that he was taking her to his village. "No," she said quietly, "You go if it's time for you to go, but I'm staying." Storm's body tensed, then he replied, just as quietly, "No, you will come with me." As he finished speaking he stood up and went to the door. Angry and offended, she raised her voice and clearly told him she was not going with him. Just who did he think he was?

Storm knew he made the right decision to take her to his medicine women. Every time he had to brush and braid her hair or touch her in any way he seemed to hurt her. Sometimes when he combed her hair he was too rough and Moon Beam cried out in pain and anger. He tried to be gentle with the brush but he couldn't concentrate because he wanted to bury his face into her hair instead. He had never felt anything so soft and silky. Yes, he must take her to the medicine women before he did something that he'd be sorry for. How damned pathetic he was, he was smitten right down to her feet. When he helped her with her slippers he had the strongest urge to caress those delicate feet. But he didn't, because he could well imagine her reaction.

At times he wanted to tell her that when she had learned her place he'd take her for his woman. But somewhere deep inside he knew that would be the biggest mistake of his life, even if he said it in jest.

Storm calmly readied one of the horses the braves

had left for him. Shadow and the pack were off hunting. The other packs had left for their own territories once they had seen that their Great Wolf was still alive. This was a good thing. The less wolves there were the less he would have to worry about. He knew that if she were struggling when he took her away, he would be putting his life in danger. The wolves would come to her defence immediately if she cried out. He attempted to coax the horse over to him. Storm and Moon Beam were going to have to ride double on the other horse if Black wouldn't come willingly. Storm didn't want to do this because they could cover more ground in less time if they were on two horses. Storm felt bad about what he was planning to do, but he knew she wouldn't go with him without a fight. He also knew that, in order to get Moon Beam up on Black, it would have to be done without a struggle. If the horse sensed any reluctance they wouldn't be going anywhere.

Storm knew the wolves preferred the evening hunt because that's when the deer begin to move around. After the last wolf had disappeared Storm made his move. But, for some uncanny reason, just as he headed for the cabin Shadow wandered back into the area. He walked over to the horse and stood there. Storm cursed, the wolf clearly suspected something. Storm thought about this and asked himself what he had usually been doing this time of the day ... getting water and wood for the night of course. That was it. So he busied himself while Shadow watched for a few minutes, and then, deciding nothing was amiss he turned and left. However, he hesitated occasionally and looked back. The wolf had sensed that things weren't quite right. Just then Fawn came back to get him, he looked back toward the cabin one more time, then turned and trotted along behind Fawn. Then, with a yip they disappeared into the bush. He wouldn't be back till morning, which would give Storm a good ten-hour start. Storm slowly let out his breath and slowly walked to the cabin. In his hands he held some rope and a piece of cloth. This wasn't going to be easy and it wasn't going to be fun. He wished he didn't have to do it this way.

Moon Beam awoke as he put the gag over her mouth. Her hands were bound. She tried to kick out with her good leg but Storm calmly moved out of her way. She felt a searing pain and after a very brief and feeble struggle she simply passed out. Storm hurried to gather her clothes and her brushes tying them in a deer hide. Then, almost in tears, he picked Moon Beam up and gently packed her out to the horses. Black knew something was wrong but he could smell her and sensed that she wasn't in any danger. After all, she had looked like this all through that terrible ride to the cabin. The big horse snorted a few times but gave in to Storm's will. He knew Storm had rescued her and was somehow bonded to the girl. Storm calmly tied Moon Beam onto the horse, talking softly all the while. He told Black her new name, and said it gently over and over.

Once he was sure Moon Beam couldn't fall off he tied her belongings on his own horse and they started out. Storm knew Moon Beam was pretty weak but he was disturbed that she was still out cold. They would have to travel fast and with as few breaks as possible because he wanted to stay ahead of the wolves. It wouldn't take the big wolf long to figure out that the horse was gone, and if the horses were gone he'd know Moon Beam was gone. Storm realized that, from the time Shadow was a pup, the horse and the girl had never left him behind. And when the wolf started following their trail he would be travelling at a much faster pace than the two horses. If he caught up with them that would likely be the end of the trip. Storm knew that he had to make it to the village for Moon Beam's sake. He didn't know what more could be done for her, but the women in his village would.

They were about an hour or two away when Storm stopped. Moon Beam had regained consciousness. He quietly told her he wanted to take the cloth off her mouth but that she had to promise she wouldn't scream or whistle for the wolves. Gently reassuring her, he told her that he couldn't fix what was wrong with her, but that the women in his village could. He assured her that he would tell his people that the wolves were coming and that they must not harm them. He gave his word that he would return her to her home when she was healed. But he warned her that if she screamed or struggled he would have to put the gag back on.

Moon Beam nodded her head. She hurt too much to fight, besides, she didn't really know if she wanted to fight. She did know there was something seriously wrong with her and that she really did need help. If he kept his word and let the wolves come to her it would be okay. But if he didn't he would pay dearly. She knew that her wolves would fight till the last one lay dead if they couldn't get to her.

CHAPTER 12

A Tumultuous Relationship

Storm made it to the village with a very tired and sick Moon Beam. He immediately called out to the braves to come quickly, that he had something important to tell them. Storm told them to keep the women, children, and dogs inside until the wolves had a chance to be with Moon Beam. He estimated that the wolves would arrive very soon, as he could hear the howling in the distance. They had made it to the village just in time.

Shadow was coming in fast, faster than even Storm had anticipated. The wolf was frantic as he followed the scent of Black. He was determined to find the girl and if the Indian stood in his way the wolf would tear his throat out. The wolves stopped just outside the village. Shadow howled and listened, a flurry of weak whistles responded. Storm was wondering what Moon Beam was telling the wolves. Wolves surrounded the village and he was hoping his people would do as had ordered and that they wouldn't panic. He listened again as more whistles and howls were exchanged. She was telling Shadow, Wind, and Bolt to enter the village but to leave the rest of the wolves where they were.

Shadow led the way in with Wind and Bolt following. Black, who Storm had released as soon as he had lifted Moon Beam off his back, had already gone out to meet the wolves. Shadow tentatively entered the teepee to greet Moon Beam but when Storm moved toward them he snarled. He had started to trust the man but now he wasn't sure. The big wolf stood over Moon Beam where she lay on a pallet. Wind and Bolt had just entered the teepee but stood back, watching. Shadow was tired from running as were the rest of the pack. He had rarely been parted from the girl before, and then only for the hunt.

He'd been confused when he returned to the cabin, and it had taken him only a moment to realize she was gone. Shadow had never been afraid of another animal. His creed was to kill or be killed. But when he realized that she was nowhere to be found, he had panicked. He was suddenly afraid, and as though he were a small pup, a wave of loneliness washed over him. This great wolf, with his impressive size and strength, did not know that much of his courage had come from this young girl who loved and protected him. From a small defenceless pup to the giant he had become the girl had been his life. Never again would he go on a hunt and leave her behind without one of the pack to watch over her. Never again did he want experience this feeling of total abandonment and loneliness.

Wind and Bolt came in close to the girl once Shadow stepped back and sat. Moon Beam cradled their big heads in her hands. Storm watched her, wondering what she was telling them. He knew they were communicating from the low hand signals and the weak but determined voice coming from her, and the soft growls of response from the wolves. The horse stood at the entrance of the teepee listening, patiently waiting for the wolves to come out.

Storm was proud of his people. None of them came out of their teepees or made a sound, other than the sound of a crying infant. Even the dogs were quiet. They were probably being fed bits of meat to keep them occupied. After several minutes the wolves turned to leave. But suddenly, standing there blocking their way was a huge village dog. Storm was horrified. Suddenly, the dog leaped for Shadow's throat. There was a furious blur of fur and Shadow grabbed the dog by the neck. The dog tried to break free of the wolf but lost his footing and fell. Shadow started shaking him by the throat. The girl whistled on hearing the commotion. Shadow dropped the dog and stepped away from him. The dog was motionless. Shadow turned his head to the side, whined, and looked quizzically at Moon Beam. She had never interfered with a kill or a fight before. She motioned with her hand and he ran back to her. As she hugged him to her, she whispered, "It's okay Shadow, it's okay." Storm watched with amazement as the village dog stayed down, seeming to know that if he twitched he was dead. Wind and Bolt stood by him daring him to move. Meanwhile, the horse had been very agitated and had wanted to trample the dog himself, but he wasn't always as quick to act as the big wolf was.

Shadow licked Moon Beam's face then turned to leave. Storm asked if the wolves were going home. She looked at Storm, said "No" and lay back down, then turned away and closed her eyes.

Storm abruptly turned and stomped out, frustrated. He did not understand her and could not believe she had just dismissed him with no explanation at all. Just when he thought she was beginning to trust him she shut him out and made him feel as worthless as a flea on a dog. Storm looked around outside the teepee to see what the wolves were doing. Only the horse remained close to the opening. The injured dog was still lying on the ground. Storm nudged it with his foot and snarled, "Get up, you're not dead."

The horse left a few times to graze nearby but always came right back to the teepee and stood guard, like a sentry, staring off into the distance. He'd whinny to Moon Beam on his return and she would whisper something to him. It didn't take Storm long to figure out that he had been assigned to watch over her. Black made it hard for the women to come in to look after Moon Beam. They were, understandably, afraid of him. Storm had to tell her to ask the horse to back off from the doorway so the women could come and go. The only one he freely let in was Storm.

The wolves stayed out of sight, except for Shadow, Wind, and Bolt were just outside the camp within whistling distance of Moon Beam. Knowing the wolves were that close unnerved the village dogs and they were unusually restless, but they stayed out of the wolves' way, nervously letting them come and go.

Every evening at sundown Moon Beam talked to them with a succession of whistles and a lone wolf would answer, driving the dogs wild. They would bark and yelp running from one end of the village to the other. To everyone's amusement, the dogs demon-strated their bravery only within the perimeter of the village.

Moon Beam was doing remarkably well under the constant care of the women who bathed her and tended to her leg. The different herbs and medicines they made for her were definitely helping and Moon Beam knew it. Her headaches, which were the most debilitating of her pains, were gradually subsiding, and the severe pain in her side was now less frequent. As things settled down, Moon Beam didn't see much of Storm during the day, but he always came just before sundown to help her up and, once her leg was healed enough, to take her for short walks outside.

Moon Beam was always glad to see him when he walked through the flap of the teepee. He always greeted her kindly, but he never smiled. He just reached down and took her hands in his to help her up. Sometimes their eyes met and Storm would try to hold her gaze but she usually looked away. She was afraid of his intensity and it seemed as if she was powerless in his presence. Often, she felt like hiding when he looked at her like that. In her naiveté, she failed to recognize his look of desire and he couldn't always hide it.

Moon Beam found the inside of the teepee very interesting and she was impressed at the skill involved in managing the smoke from the fire. The fire pit was in the centre of the teepee and was about a foot-and-a-half across and a few inches deep. A canvas stretched between two or three poles in front of the opening reached to the ground. This made the draught rise behind it towards the vent at the top of the teepee. The Indians made a circular bell boat of rawhide on a frame of willows as a storm cap on top of the teepee to stop the rain or snow from coming inside. If the wind blew from the west they set both smoke flaps with the poles pointing east and all the smoke would go out the vent. If the wind changed to the south they would drop the north smoke flaps and swing the south smoke pole till it pointed north. If the wind blew from the east they closed the smoke flaps on each other and left the door open and the smoke would go out that way.

Around the inner edge of the teepee were sleeping mats with several hides. The cooking utensils were kept close to the fire. Along one section of the inner edge there were piles of neatly folded clothing and on another section were the fleshing bones used to clean the hides as well as hooks and bone needles for sewing. Moon Beam loved it. Everything had a place and the teepee was always kept very tidy. So this is how the Indians lived, she mused. She had always wondered what the inside of a teepee looked like. Moon Beam found the children happy and welcoming and enjoyed watching them play. Aside from the wolves, Moon Beam had never had playmates. In fact this was the first time in her life she had been exposed to children.

During this time Moon Beam discovered that Swift Fawn, the beautiful Indian woman she had rescued during the violent assault, was one of Storm's sisters, and the child who she had saved from drowning was Fawn's child. Moon Beam had been told that he had three sisters but no brothers. She had thought that the child she had saved that day was Storm's child, but now the relationship was clear. His other sisters' names were Morning Dove and Evening Mist, and his mother and father were called Morning Dew and Flying Hawk.

Moon Beam thought Storm and his father were as different as night and day. Flying Hawk was carefree and easygoing where Storm was rigid and stern. One day she had a disagreement with Storm within his father's hearing. After Storm had stomped away angry, Flying Hawk came in to talk to her about it and told her that Storm had always taken life and himself too seriously.

The men in the village treated Moon Beam with great respect because all of them recognized what great warriors she and her wolves were. This annoyed Storm to no end. He remembered how helpless he had been and how a woman had saved him and protected him, and this bothered him. Storm was constantly torn between love and jealousy. As long as Moon Beam agreed and did exactly what he wanted they got along just fine. But when she disagreed with him he would usually leave in a fit of anger.

As for Moon Beam, she was thoroughly frustrated. She didn't know how to act when he was around. It seemed that he disapproved of everything she said and did. Sometimes Flying Hawk would shake his head. He didn't know why his son was being so hard on her and he didn't like it, especially as the girl minded her own business and kept to herself. She was never rude or boastful, which would have been an affront to any Indian man. And, for the most part, she seemed to respect Storm. She never argued with him, but when she'd had enough of his belligerence and rudeness she would just shut him out. At times like this, Moon Beam couldn't wait till she was well enough to get out of there and away from him.

Other times, Moon Beam liked to watch him ride through the village as he came in from hunting. He was an awesome man, fearless, strong, and very sure of himself. His headdress made him look unapproachable, almost cruel. As he rode in he would look around, his eyes missing nothing. His bare upper body was strong and his muscular arms rippled as he controlled his horse. His shoulders were broad and, strangely, the terrible scars on his back added to his attraction.

With his bow hung over his torso, his hatchet tied to his left side, and his huge hunting knife in a sheath on his right side, he was definitely someone one you would want on your side. Moon Beam noticed how the young women doted on him and went out of their way to attract his attention. She also noticed that most the attention seeking seemed to annoy him. She shook her head. The man just couldn't relax and enjoy himself, even if he wanted to.

CHAPTER 13

The Whiteman's Ultimatum

Moon Beam had been in the Indian village for almost two months when two Whitemen arrived in the village. One of the men had a great mop of red hair, and had freckles splattered across his nose. He was average in height with broad shoulders, and introduced himself as Jim Taylor. The other man was tall and lean with curly blonde hair and said his name was Sid Boyer. They were government surveyors and had come to survey crown land for Britain. The tribe was told that their village, and its surrounding twenty thousand acres of land, belonged to the Crown. The land was about to be auctioned off to settlers arriving from the east. Unless they could come up with $200 an acre their land would be sold to the settlers, and the Indians would have to move elsewhere.

Storm was angry, his first thought being to slit the throats of these two Whitemen. He knew better though. The soldiers would come. And many of his people would die. There were at least two hundred children in his village, what would happen to them if their fathers were killed? And where would the others go? They would have to find another tribe to taken them in, and that would be almost impossible. How could a queen own the land? Not only did she live across the ocean and had never even seen this land, but now this woman chief wanted to take it from them. Besides, no one owned the land, no man, no animal, and certainly no woman. This was Indian Territory, theirs to live and die on. The Great Spirit had given it to them centuries ago and it couldn't be sold or traded. The surveyors informed them that if they did not comply, the soldiers would come and enforce the Crown's will.

Moon Beam, who had been standing back listening to the two men walked up to them. Both men were surprised to see a white woman in an Indian camp and even more surprised when she introduced herself. She offered no explanation for her presence other than that she was recovering from an accident. She asked the two men to come and sit by her teepee and have something to eat. Storm walked away, seething.

As they ate they pulled out their maps to show Moon Beam the boundaries of the land that was about to be offered for sale. Moon Beam noted from the map that the Indian village was clearly marked as Carcajou. About another one hundred and twenty miles north, following the river marked on the map, was Fort Vermillion, then further on another Indian village.

Moon Beam, whose mother and father had taught her to read and to understand maps, inquired about her own valley, which was also marked on the map, "What about this valley?" Her heart fell as they told her that it too was crown land. But her father had homesteaded on it and now it was her home. How could these officious Whitemen come in and take it away from her? How could they take the home of Storm's people away? They had lived on this land for centuries.

Moon Beam pointed to her valley and asked how many acres it was. The men weren't sure but guessed it would be at least fifteen thousand acres. She asked them why the price was so high, "Isn't $200 a lot of money per acre?" Her father sometimes talked about the price of land. Jim looked at Sid and Sid hung his head so he wouldn't have to look her in the eye.

Jim finally replied, "The truth of the matter is the government knows about this prime land and the resources that come with it. Frankly, this is their way of forcing the Indians out. They know the Indians can't come up with that kind of money. They are going to bring the settlers in and sell the land to them for fifteen dollars an acre." "It's not right and it's not fair," Sid added, "but that's the way it is."

"Where does a person go if they want to buy land?" she asked. Sid told her that there was an office called the Land Office in the town of Peace River. They showed her their surveyor's map and told her how to get to the town.

Meanwhile Storm, who was standing with his braves discussing the situation, was seething. How dare she invite these strangers to her teepee when he was talking to them? It was not the place of a woman to invite them to her dwelling and offer them food. Storm was now convinced that this impetuous one had no understanding of proper social behaviour. And she had humiliated him by turning her back on him in from of these men.

Moon Beam, not realizing that she had deeply insulted Storm, carried on talking to the two men, intent on getting as much information out of them as possible. Conversation was something she had only experienced with her parents.

Storm could hardly contain himself. This woman needed to be taught a lesson, once and for all, about a woman's place. She seemed to be oblivious to the unspoken roles acted out by men and women. Her and her damned wolves, he wished that he had never laid eyes on them. They had turned his life upside down. Even his people seemed to be living their lives around this woman and her animals. She acted as if she were a man's equal and that she had the right to do anything she wanted to. It was infuriating. Had she no morals? No discipline? Sometimes he wondered whether she'd *ever* had a mother and father. Maybe wolves had raised her. No that couldn't be, she didn't even understand about male dominance in the animal kingdom. Storm wasn't thinking very clearly.

Moon Beam had been on her own with her wolves for a long time. She didn't even realize that some human beings might think that they were superior to others or that they could order another person around. As far as Moon Beam was concerned nobody owned her, just like nobody owned the wolves, they were free to come and go as they pleased.

After a while, Jim and Sid went back to join the men and continued talking through the evening and well into the night, leaving Moon Beam on her own. At this point she was glad she had the opportunity to plan how she was going to get back to her valley and make plans to protect the wolves. She had to think of a way to permanently keep their territory safe. It looked like a trip to the town she had heard so much about from her father was going to be necessary.

Before Sid and Jim left Moon Beam had one more question for them. She brought out one of the nuggets she had found in the stream. Since her find in the stream that day she had carried a small one around for good luck. Years ago her father had shown her a piece like this and told her it was gold. She asked them if it was gold and how much it was worth. They figured probably about $200 to $250 dollars, maybe even $300, as gold was pretty scarce in this part of the country.

CHAPTER 14

A Bad Move and a Disturbing Parting

The next day, after the men were gone, Moon Beam started gathering her belongings. Her plan was to slip away in the night, meet up with her wolves, and be gone before anyone noticed. After the evening meal the village, as usual, became quiet. Here and there you could hear the children laughing or a baby fussing. The low voices of the adults discussing their day were peaceful to Moon Beam's ears. She was enjoying the quiet of the evening when Storm appeared. As he stepped inside Moon Beam got up to greet him but he did something unusual that unnerved her. He closed the flap on the door.

Moon Beam knew something was wrong as she looked up at him. His jaw was set as if he was gritting his teeth and his dark eyes were flashing black. Moon Beam instinctively stepped back from him, but he reached out and grabbed her arm pulling her against him. He demanded to know why she rudely interrupted him when he was talking to the Whitemen.

Then, with quiet but unsettling determination, he announced, "If anyone talks about the problems of this village it is the chief, not some other man, and especially not a woman. You don't seem to know your place. I think it's time for you to learn what a woman's place is."

Moon Beam was amazed and, believing she had done nothing wrong, she tried to pull away from him. Storm just held her tighter and said ... "And I'm going to show you." Holding her with one arm and holding the back of her head with the other he suddenly and roughly pressed his lips to hers. She couldn't breathe and she panicked. His lips and body were commanding hers to bend to his will. Moon Beam fought to free herself from his lips so she could whistle for her wolves, but Storm had anticipated this. With his lips pressed tight it was impossible to her to call them. She wasn't going to get the best of him this time.

His softened a little but he held her tight. Moon Beam suddenly felt as though her body had turned to water and had no substance at all. If Storm hadn't been holding her she would have fallen down, her legs seemed to have turned to jelly. What was happening to her?

Storm sensed her responsiveness. What had started out in anger had ended in overwhelming passion. At one point, Storm pulled away trying to stop his out-of-control feelings. Now that he had forced her respond to him, he was suddenly afraid of his own overwhelming emotions. But Moon Beam moaned and pulled him back to her, her young and innocent body crying out to be fulfilled. Only Storm could fill the void she began to feel when she sensed that he was trying to pull away from her.

Moon Beam didn't move for a long time after. Later, she couldn't believe what had happened. Her body had betrayed her as she responded to his passionate lovemaking. As she gradually stopped resisting he became gentle and her body took over her mind. When he felt he was close to being out of control he suddenly held back. But Moonbeam pulled him to her and then he no longer had control. He didn't want to stop, and he surrendered to her will.

By the time her quivering subsided, Moon Beam had convinced herself that he had forced her. She had read things about situations like this. She was appalled believed there should be no forgiveness for it. She hated him in that moment, but she hated herself even more because she had resisted being in his arms, until her body betrayed her and passionately responded to him. She was utterly confused

Where were her wolves when she needed them? If she could have whistled they would have come to protect her — even if it was from herself. Moon Beam decided that men were a problem, they were totally puzzling to her, except for her father. She just couldn't understand when she tried to compare Storm's manner and actions to her father's gentle and loving nature.

Moon Beam lay there for quite awhile, thinking about all that had happened over the past year, and then made a decision. She gathered her few possessions

together and crept stealthily outside. Once she was
past the perimeter of the sleeping village, she softly
whistled for Black. Within seconds he was at her side
and Moon Beam swung up on his back, forgetting all
about her bad leg. It felt wonderful, until she gripped
her horse's sides with her thighs and realized just how
weak and painful her leg still was. She awkwardly
pressed Black's side with her good leg and in a few
minutes they were far from the village.

Moon Beam whistled for the wolves and then
dismounted to wait in the dark for them. When she
heard them coming, she gave another whistle and
Shadow immediately answered. They greeted her
joyfully, bouncing around like puppies, but in the
dark she couldn't tell them apart. Except for Shadow
because he was so big, and Bolt because he always
came up with his head under her hand. Moon Beam
was elated. It had been roughly two months with only
sporadic visits from her family of furry friends. She
was overjoyed to be back with them. "Okay Shadow,
take us home, Black will follow you, and I am just
going to enjoy the ride home and ignore the pain."
And she did. A little before dawn Moon Beam pushed
Black into a run. She couldn't wait to get home.

When Storm awoke in the morning he covered his
head with his hands. What had he done? He had gone
to her in a fit of anger. He was aware of his temper
and he knew that when it was unleashed someone
usually ended up either dead or badly hurt. He had
been angry over the Whiteman's threat to take away
his people's tribal land, because he was powerless to

prevent it from happening. He was frustrated because he was afraid he couldn't save his village. Not without starting a war to fight for it — a war he knew they would lose.

He had taken his frustration and fury out on Moon Beam. At least it had started that way. Among his people there was punishment for forcing oneself on a woman against her will. Storm pulled himself from his bed, repulsed by his actions. He couldn't undo what he had done but maybe she would listen to him. Maybe he could straighten things out. He would ask her to be his woman.

As he walked to Moon Beam's teepee he tried to think of how to approach her. He knew he had gone too far and too fast. How could he explain his jealousy at watching her laugh with and talk to those men? The pain of watching her throw her head back in laughter with them when she rarely bothered to talk to him, had been more than he could bear. He had seen the way her beautiful eyes lit up when they talked of the Whiteman's town. How could he have explained to her how he felt every time they were together? She always kept him at arms length no matter what he did. It seemed so unfair. The one woman he wanted didn't seem to care about him at all, and the women he didn't care about gave him as much pleasure as black flies.

As he reached the teepee he knew something was amiss because he couldn't see Black anywhere. His heart fell to his feet when he opened the flap. She was gone. There was no way he could explain his love for her or show her how sorry he was. He could follow her but she was with the pack now and, after last night, if she knew he was following she would surely set the wolves on him. Storm recalled how she and her wolves had not hesitated to kill those men who were brutalizing his sister. He also remembered the shock he felt when it was over. He had looked into Moon Beam's eyes — and they were as cold as a wolf's eyes after a kill.

He decided to wait a couple of days and then go after her. That would give her time to settle down. He knew what she could do with a bow and arrow, or a knife, or a hatchet if she had a mind to. Besides, surrounded by her wolves her dwelling place would be a fortress for the first few days.

CHAPTER 15

An Unforgettable Trip to the Bank

As soon as Moon Beam reached the cabin she started preparing for the trip to the town of Peace River. She went to the door of the secret room where all the gold was hidden and began to figure out how many nuggets she would have to take with her. Assuming there was thirty-five thousand acres of land at $200 an acre she would need $7 million dollars to buy all the land. When she asked Sid and Jim how much money one would need to buy that much land they thought she would need at least twenty-eight thousand nuggets at $250 per nugget. By this time both the men and Moon Beam laughed out loud, the men at how impossible it would be for one person to have that much money, and Moon Beam because she had so many nuggets she didn't know what to do with them.

Now she had to figure out how to get all the gold to town. She estimated she would have to make at least six trips carrying almost five thousand nuggets each trip. She knew she must be careful not to attract

any unnecessary attention to herself and her travelling companions, the wolves. Her plan was to bury
the nuggets from each trip a few miles from the town.
Once she had all of the gold that close she would go
into Peace River and buy a wagon and a couple of
horses, load the gold, and pull it into town to the bank.

In the end it took Moon Beam two-and-a-half
months to move the gold to town as it ended up
taking eleven trips instead of six. The gold proved
to be much too heavy to take five thousand nuggets
each time. Moon Beam was greatly amused when all
the nuggets she took from her hidden cache didn't
seem to make much of a dent in the gold still in there.
It got Moon Beam wondering just how much gold she
did have, and how much it was worth.

When Moon Beam first rode into town she looked
around to see where the bank was, and if there was a
sheriff in the town. She then went to the stables to see
if she could negotiate the use of a wagon and horses.
After selecting a good sturdy wagon with big horses,
she told the stableman she needed a canvas to cover
her goods. She gave the man a small nugget for pay-
ment. "Hey little lady, where did you get this?" the
weary man asked, "Do you have any more?" Moon
Beam said, "No. It was given it to me by my father
before he died." "Well, lucky me," the man said, "My
name is Bill and I'm also Blacksmith here in town."
Moon Beam introduced herself and asked him if he
knew where the Land Office was. Then she asked him.
"If you had lots of gold, where would you take it?" Bill
threw back his head and laughed, saying, "I'd take it

straight to the bank because they have scales right there. It keeps everybody honest and, since I have the only nugget for miles around, that's where I'm heading right now. I'm pretty sure you'll have some change coming." Moon Beam nodded. There was no sense in making him think she might have money to throw around. When the team was all hitched up, Moon Beam tied Black to the back of the wagon and waved goodbye to Bill as she left. She told him that she would have the team back to him sometime in the next day or two.

Once Moon Beam left town and was well out of sight, she instructed the wolves to guard the road. They would stay there until she returned to the isolated and heavily treed place where she'd buried the gold. Nobody had followed her, even though there was fair amount of curiosity about her and her huge horse, which quietly followed the wagon without being tied to it. They wondered about the wagon, but maybe she was bringing goods into town or needed to move something. No one had any idea where she came from.

Moon Beam, who was unusually strong for her size and build, slowly loaded the gold and covered it with the canvas. When she was finished she sat down and ate what was left of the food she had brought. After some time, she headed back to town with the heavily burdened wagon and labouring horses. As the wagon pulled up to the bank Moon Beam was wondering what her next move should be. She really didn't know, so she climbed down off the wagon and walked confidently into the bank. It was a small pleasant room with a big counter, and further back in a smaller room she could see the safe, as well as a desk full of papers with a young man hunched over them. She figured that they must not have much money in this bank, everything being in such a small space. In another corner of the room were the weigh scales.

Moon Beam asked the lady behind the little counter if she could see the boss. The lady asked her for her name and if she had ever been in before. She laughed and told the woman her name was Rachel Ressler and that, no, she had not been in before. What she didn't tell the woman was that she was nineteen years old and this was her first trip to civilization.

A minute or two later the handsome young bank manager came walking towards her. She was surprised because she had expected an old man. He introduced himself as Dean Young and asked what he could do for her. As he looked at her, he noted her beautiful buckskin dress and the modest curves beneath it. Her long white hair hung down to her waist making him think about what it would be like to run his fingers through it. Her dark brown eyes and delicate features made him want to stand there and just look at her. He had seen beautiful women before but none of them compared to this one.

Dean gave himself a shake to focus on what she was saying and she introduced herself as Rachel Ressler. She asked him if they could speak in private outside the door by her wagon, as she wanted to show him something. Once outside by the wagon, she said,

"I want your vow of complete secrecy about what I am going to show you and what I want you to do. I want no attention drawn to this wagon and I know you will want the same thing. We will need privacy and secrecy in this matter."

Dean was intrigued and chuckled softly. He couldn't imagine what was so important to her that she had to create all this drama. Oh well, he'd play along with her, besides he might get a chance to get acquainted with this beauty.

Rachel told him what was under the canvas and that she wanted him to have it packed into the bank for weighing after the bank closed for the evening. She told him she had stored the gold in big bags of hide and that they were concealed so that no one would know what was in them. She mentioned that it would be a good thing if there were another man he could trust to help. Dean nodded his head nonchalantly. But once he saw for himself what was under the wrappings, he was in a slight state of shock. Dean called to the lady behind the counter to tell her that he was going out for a bit.

Then Rachel and the bank manager walked a few doors down the wooden sidewalk to the Sheriff's Office. Dean introduced her to the sheriff. His name was John Kane and Rachel liked him and trusted him right away. He was a swarthy-looking man with a kindly face, but his eyes could look right through people and give him a sense of whether or not they were honest. John Kane was seldom wrong in his assumptions about people. But all that he could tell about Rachel was that she was "babe-in-the-woods" who didn't have a dishonest bone in her body. "Okay," he said, "What can I do for you Rachel? She told him about the gold and what she wanted to do. He was quiet for a moment and then said, "Okay. Did you come by the gold honestly?" Rachel nodded her head telling him how it had washed down out of the river into the creek. The sheriff told her that she would have to sign a paper stating that it was hers and explaining how she had come by it. He asked if she knew the approximate value of the gold. She replied that she wasn't sure but she thought it was around $7 million. John Kane and Dean Young visibly gulped at the same time. Dean was speechless and John said, "Good God! Do you have a story for us! But first we have to unload and weigh the gold to determine how much is there." Rachel asked Dean what an ounce of gold was worth and he told her that it had been up to $425 but had recently been pegged at $400 an ounce. Rachel gulped. She was alarmed that she had brought too many nuggets, and she was hoping it would be safe in the bank. On the other hand, she wouldn't have to bring any more gold to town for a very long time.

The sheriff and the bank manager immediately sat down to work out a plan. Once they had weighed the gold, they were going to have to put it in the biggest strongboxes they had. The bank had quite a few lying around as the payroll for the men at the coalmines came in every Tuesday. The stage was due again in the morning and they wanted to make sure that all the gold was secretly weighed and stashed in the strongboxes so that it could leave immediately with the stage in the morning. If things went as planned and if luck was on their side, news of the unusually large gold shipment would not get around, at least not until the stagecoach left again.

When the bank closed and dusk settled over the town, the three of them hauled the gold into the bank through a well-treed backyard door. After weighing and marking the gold they put it into the strong-boxes. It took hours, and when they were finished around dawn there were seventeen boxes of gold. The gold would be shipped to Edmonton where the big gold centre was. It would be safe there, they assured her. When it was all said and done Rachel had $19 million in the little bank in the town of Peace River.

The stagecoach arrived as expected at exactly eight o'clock in the morning. After they quickly unloaded the cargo, the seventeen strongboxes were loaded onto the stagecoach. The only unusual thing early risers noticed was that, instead of four horses were pulling the stage when it came in, six were harnessed and pulling it when it left. Once the stage drove out of sight the sheriff, the young bank manager, and Rachel all heaved a sigh of relief.

"Well little lady," the Sheriff said, "You must be ready for some breakfast. Let's go over to the hotel and you can fill us in on the story of the gold while we eat. First off though, I'd like to know where a little thing like you and your big horse came from."

Rachel explained to the Sheriff about her father

and mother's deaths. She also told them how it was that she and Black stuck together through this very difficult time and how much it changed their lives when she found the wolf cubs. She told him about the Indian village and the surveyors who came to chase the Indians off the land. The sheriff became very white and then, quietly, he asked her what her father's name was. When she told him it was Morgan Ressler, the sheriff gasped and choked on the mouthful of coffee he'd just taken in. After he got his breath back his eyes widened and he whispered in a low intense voice," What? Did I hear you correctly? Did you say Morgan Ressler? Rachel stood up, afraid that she had said something wrong. Taken aback and afraid her father's name had upset the sheriff, she hesitated, and then said in a quiet voice, "I said Morgan Ressler."

He immediately jumped up, "My Lord child! Was your mother's name Brittany?" "Yes," said Rachel, "it was." And in an instant he was on her side of the table picking her up in his arms and swinging her around. The people in the little diner all stopped eating to listen to what was going on. He put her down in front of him and said, "Your mother's name was Brittany Kane. She's my sister! I'm your bloody uncle, that's what I am!"

Rachel was dazed ... how could this be? Her mother was from the east. She had known that she had a couple of uncles, but presumed them to be back east where her mother came from. "But, how did you end up here in Peace River so far from your home?"

she asked. He put her back in her chair and sat down, saying, "Your father and mother disappeared about ten years after they were married. The letters had been few and far between, maybe once a year one would arrive. When they stopped completely your grandmother insisted that one of us come out here and look for them. The last letter they sent was from was a place called Peace River. So that's how I ended up here. I looked for a couple of years and couldn't find anybody who could remember them. After some time we decided that they must be dead. I liked it here and they needed a sheriff. So I took the job and I've been here ever since."

Rachel couldn't believe her ears. Dean sat there in stunned silence with his mouth open, his head turning back and forth with the conversation. It was unbelievable. Rachel was speechless — still reeling from the sheriff's story — her *uncle's* story. Of course, he wanted to know everything. She started by telling him, "That's why I'm here Uncle ... should I call you Uncle? "Hell yes girl! I am your uncle!" Rachel hesitated, conscious of those around her, and then she lowered her voice to a whisper and said, "Uncle John, I *have* to save the valley, Sunny Valley. It was my father's valley."

She told them she wanted to go to the Land Office so she could buy the thirty-five thousand acres. Both her newly found uncle and Dean Kane were spellbound as she filled them in. They knew her incredulous story must be true. They had seen the gold and they knew how much the girl was worth.

Rachel didn't have the heart to tell them that back home there was even more gold. The two men just presumed that what they had packed up and shipped was all the gold there was.

After they finally got back to their breakfasts and finished eating, the three of them casually walked over to the Land Office. Rachel was grateful that they were with her. Without them, who would believe that an unaccompanied young woman, a complete stranger, could have enough money to buy thousands of acres of land?

They introduced her to Nels Gibson who ran the Land Office for the Crown. He told her that he had previously been a mapmaker and draftsman. But he liked this job a whole lot better, he told them, because he got to know people and all about their business and about their comings and goings. After listening to her highly unusual request, he went to get the appropriate land maps. Rachel showed him the land on the map that she wanted to purchase. He was familiar with both areas as there had been much talk of forcing the Indians out and selling the prime land to settlers. People didn't agree with the government's devious plan. But how could simple honest people fight the government or the Crown?

Nels became noticeably excited when Rachel explained exactly what she wanted to do. One title was made out to Rachel Ressler on behalf of Storm's people, with him named as their chief, because if the Crown was really after the land they might not let the Indians buy it (even if they had the means). The government wanted to fill it with settlers and get rid of the Indians. Treaty 8 wasn't signed until 1898, so the Indians could own land only as long as they occupied the land the Crown had "given" them. But if they moved off of the land they automatically lost it. Many Indians lost their land by selling it to the rich Europeans who came from over the sea.

The Land Office issued one title for twenty-two thousand acres at $200 per acre for $4,400,000. The other title was for seventeen thousand acres of land in the valley at $200 an acre for $3,400,000. Rachel walked out with two land titles for a total cost of $7,800,000 — "Paid in Full." Once everything was signed, sealed, and delivered with a bank draft the four of them decided to call it a day.

So much had happened in those twenty-four hours that the sheriff announced he was heading for home and bed. Dean offered to find accommodation for Rachel. Uncle John asked her when she would be leaving, as he didn't want to miss seeing her before she left town. She assured him she wouldn't leave without seeing him first. Rachel planned on getting some rest and then buying a few things at the general store the next day. As she would only have Black to transport them, she wouldn't be able to take much.

Dean accompanied her to a small boarding house where she got a bed for the night. He asked the landlady to send the bill for the room and three meals to the bank. He also pointed out the direction of the General Store. Then Dean kissed her hand and bid her goodnight. She was a little startled by the act because she had never experienced this kind of thing before. Oh, yes, she had read about the practice in books but she wasn't clear about the intent of the nicety, and it had taken her off guard. Dean left for his boarding house walking on air.

The landlady offered to make Rachel a hot meal and to draw a bath for her, which she gratefully accepted. Although she was more hungry than tired, the idea of bathing in warm water was very appealing. She was sore all over. Later, as she climbed into bed, and between two sheets for the first time in her life, she thought about how strange her situation was and how different it was from anything she had ever experienced. Then she jumped up and opened the window as wide as it would go.

Before going to sleep she thought about her next move and decided she would have to stay another night. She had something very important to do. She knew the wolves would take care of themselves and not come traipsing into town to look for her. Not yet anyway, although the thought amused her considerably.

First thing the next morning Dean went over to the General Store and told the proprietor about Rachel. He asked him to send bills for her purchases to the bank and told the man that the bank would be handling all her affairs. Dean knew the girl was a highly intelligent person but he also knew that she had no idea about money. It was going to take her some time to learn about these matters and he felt compelled to protect her.

The next morning, after a hefty breakfast, she ran into Bill, the Blacksmith, on the street. She told him she had stayed in town for the night and asked him if she could buy the wagon and team from him. "You bet you can," he said. You already have. I had my nugget weighed and I got almost $400 for it. Rent on the wagon and team would only have amounted to $10, even if you kept them three days. And it's been great doing business with you!" Rachel asked if he could take the team back to his stable to water and feed them and keep them overnight. He agreed and she told him she'd come around the next day and pick them up.

In the morning Rachel was up early as she had lots to do before she left town. She had heard that a baby had been born the day before and that a woman, a neighbour, had helped the mother with the birth. She also heard that this woman helped deliver most of the babies in and around the town. Rachel wanted to see her, as she had a strong feeling that she might be pregnant. Besides, she desperately wanted to talk to another woman.

Damn Storm! She never had any intentions of having a baby, let alone having one forced on her. The wolves were trouble enough and much more fun. She had just never thought of herself as a mother. And she wanted things to stay like they were, just her and her wolves.

It was three months since Moon Beam had left Storm back in the village, and it was now the beginning of September. If she were pregnant the baby would be born around the end of February or the beginning of March. The midwife readily confirmed her suspicions. Rachel was three months pregnant. The woman congratulated her, to Rachel's considerable embarrassment. So she was going to have a baby, an Indian baby. She could, without a doubt, strangle Storm if given a chance. At that moment, she hated him with a passion.

The midwife explained labour, emphasizing how painful it would be. Then she told Rachel all the things she would need to know and do to deliver the baby safely on her own. Rachel blanched when the woman told her how to cut and tie the umbilical cord, and that if she didn't do this, the baby would die.

Later, Rachel went shopping and bought everything a baby could possibly need, including a homemade cradle. She bought new and slightly looser clothes for herself and all kinds of groceries. She remembered the taste of sugar and flour and bought years' worth. She worried about her ability to nurse the baby. What if she didn't have enough milk? Just in case, she bought several bottles and many one-dozen boxes of canned milk.

Around one o'clock on the second day she met Bill the Blacksmith on the street and he offered to pick up her purchases and load the wagon for her when she was ready.

Rachel went to the bank to see Dean and asked him if he and her Uncle John would take care of her money. They gave her good advice. No money would be released or spent unless both of their signatures were on the note. For purchases over $30 there also had to be a note from Rachel saying what the money was to be used for. Everyone was happy. And Rachel generously offered each of them a very generous sum every month to look after her money. She still had an awful lot of money in the little bank. Maybe in a year or so she would bring the rest of the gold in and put it the bank as well.

She couldn't imagine the reactions of her Uncle John, Dean, and Nels when and if she did this, but the thought amused her. Then she went to tell her uncle about the baby. He was quiet as she told him that she was pregnant with an Indian child. He asked her if the father knew about the baby. She told him, "No, but he will … someday." He went over to her and hugged her and said, "If you're not happy in your valley I hope you will consider moving to town."

Rachel was touched by his words but, on the other hand, she wished he had told her he would like to meet her wolves someday. She had a feeling that he didn't really believe what she told him about the wolves. She asked Uncle John if he would ride with her out of town. He said that he would be honoured to, and boosted her up onto the wagon, then turned and mounted his dapple-grey horse. Horse and man seemed to suit each other she thought. Rachel and her uncle talked and visited as they rode out about a mile-and-a-half from town. Then she reined her team in, stopped, and whistled a couple of times. John was wondering what she was doing when the biggest damn wolf he had ever seen walked out of the trees towards them.

John's hand reached for his gun but Rachel said, "No Uncle John, this is Shadow," as she swung down from her wagon. The wolf was white and it was enormous. While Rachel cradled the wolf's head in her hands and began talking to it, other wolves entered the clearing and pushed their way to her side to greet her. She gave a few whistles and hand motions and the wolves started lying down. Then, she walked from wolf to wolf greeting each one individually. John couldn't believe what he was seeing. These weren't small animals, and they all must have outweighed her by at least forty pounds. But there they were, all looking at her and waiting patiently for her to acknowledge each one of them. John sat there with his mouth open, unable to speak.

John's horse was jumpy with the wolves all around so he rode him over closer to Black, which calmed it down some. John shook his head in wonder. He had never seen anything like this in his entire life. He would have to quit being sceptical about the things his niece told him. He had thought the story of the gold was a tall tale until he saw it with his own eyes. And who would believe the story about the wolves? No one.

Rachel asked her Uncle to dismount so she could introduce him to the wolves. Now the Sheriff was a brave man, but he did hesitate before getting off his horse. Rachel brought the big white wolf over to him. John held his breath as the big guy sniffed him over, and Rachel told him that the wolf would never forget his scent. "I may not be with him if you should ever meet again but once he has your scent he'll know to either let you pass or kill you." She said it so casually that John looked at her to see if she was joking. She wasn't.

She then told him that her name was Rachel all right, but only for legal purposes. Then she explained how Storm had saved her life and how he had named her Moon Beam some time after. She made it clear that she was very comfortable with her new name and that she had felt re-born after her traumatic run in with the crazed grizzly. Niece and uncle talked for a while longer and Moonbeam told him to follow the map that was in Nels' office if he ever decided to come and visit her. John hugged her, not wanting to let her go now that he had found her. He said, "You take care of yourself Moon Beam and I'll try to come in the spring. Maybe you should come back to town before the baby comes and have it here in safety." Moon Beam, not really knowing anything about having a baby, said, "Don't worry, I'll be fine." As she started off and was waving goodbye John felt the tears well up. Along with a sense of loss he was also feeling guilty as hell for letting her go off on her own, but he knew she wouldn't stay. Moon Beam was a lot like her mother, John decided, recalling that he had lost many an argument to his strong-minded sister.

As Moon Beam slowly travelled home with her loaded wagon her mind turned to the baby and Storm. She didn't need him. Maybe she would let him know he was a father after the baby was born — and then again — maybe not.

CHAPTER 16

A Difficult Birth

Storm knew where the cabin was and visited the area often. He'd wait around the cabin for two or three days at a time hoping Moonbeam would show up, but she never appeared. He suspected the wolves were warning her when he entered the valley because each time he entered it both Moon Beam and the wolves disappeared. The wolves had different lairs and she would take the things she needed for a few days and hide out with them. Storm knew there were at least two hundred wolves in that valley, but each time he showed up he'd see nary a one. He knew the wolves were watching him though, because his horse would become jumpy when the wolves were close.

Storm was pretty sure there was a baby coming because he had first noticed a bottle in the cupboard with a nipple on it. This got his attention. So he looked a little further and discovered a tiny sweater and a few other baby things hidden away on a shelf. He tried to figure out how many moons had passed since he had forced himself on her and how many more moons there would be before a baby was born. It had to be the late winter or the beginning of spring.

How could he tell her he was sorry for his behaviour that day if he never got to see her? And it was completely beyond him how he would ever be able to tell her that he couldn't stop thinking about her and that he wanted her to be his woman. Words had never come easy to him, and to top it off, he had never had to apologize to anyone for his actions. The first thing he wanted to tell her was that she could talk to anyone she pleased (even if she cut him off in mid-sentence). What he had done bothered him so much he decided to talk to his mother and tell her what had taken place. She was a wise woman and she knew about matters of the heart. He had always been able to talk to her, even after he became chief. She would know what to do.

When Morning Dew heard what he had done she looked down at her hands and said quietly, without letting him get a word in

"My son, you deserve what you've got now. Moon Beam is as wild as the wolves she runs with. She has never had to answer to anyone since she was orphaned. She is not like us. This woman is her own person and she makes her own decisions. Your father and I have watched you try to force her to do things your way. She does not know our ways. You must respect that she is different and her ways are different. We wondered how long it would be before she struck out at you. A woman will do anything she can for her man. But it is because she wants to, not because a man forces her to.

Have you ever known me, or your sisters, to remain silent when we think we are right about something? Maybe we wait until we are alone with our men to tell them what we think. But they are told when we do not agree with them. Why do you think you have the right to tell her what she can do or what she cannot do? She is not your woman. She is not even one of your tribe. You should talk to your father. He will explain respect between a man and a woman to you, and he will tell you that to get a good woman a man does not beat her or force her into his bed. You have nothing now, not the woman, not the baby she carries."

Storm looked down at his mother, and then lowered his eyes. He felt as though he were five summers old again. He stood there for a moment and then, deeply feeling his mother's disappointment in him, he turned and left her teepee. Once outside he didn't know if he felt better or worse for talking to his mother. She was disappointed in him and she had made it very clear how she felt about his actions.

The next time he returned to Moon Beam's cabin he didn't waste any time. He set to working finding and cutting firewood, even though it was considered women's work in his village, and hauled as much inside as the cabin would hold. He hauled extra water from the river in newly made birch-bark containers. Once the snow came she would be able to melt snow for water. The cabin needed new mud around the door and between the logs so the cold of winter couldn't seep in. After he did this, he cut boughs from the pine trees and piled them on the roof of the cabin for extra insulation.

As Storm worked he thought about how he had treated her. When he looked back he realized that he had been competing with her. He had been embarrassed that she could do things as well as most men could. In his mind a woman wasn't supposed to be able to think like a man. He'd always believed that women weren't capable protecting or rescuing someone. He had been completely unnerved when, without a second thought, she killed the four men who had ravaged his sister and the other two women. Retribution and revenge was something men too care of.

He thought about the ease with which she handled the wolves and the way she could ride a horse with just her knees and no reins, holding on to the mane alone. He marvelled at how she could swing herself up off the ground and land up on the horse's back when it was already into a run. There was no getting around it. She was amazing. And what was worse, there was no doubt in his mind that she was capable of doing the same things to survive as he was. He had never hesitated to kill anyone who was threatening him or his people. And what he saw in himself he saw in Moon Beam. He realized he'd been a fool.

All he wanted now was a chance to talk to her, to hear her voice once more. If only they could talk, he might be able explain himself. He vowed to treat her with respect.

If Storm felt bad that day, he felt even worse when

the surveyors came back to his village. Sid and Jim brought good news for his people. The land had been bought by a person named Rachel Ressler for the sum of $4,400,000 and gifted to Storm's tribe for as long as his people occupied the territory. Where had this money come from? How had Moon Beam managed to buy this much land? It was not possible. But there it was in the deed they gave to Storm.

Storm glared at the two men, then shrugged and walked away from them. He didn't say a word. Of course he was happy for his people and very relieved, but on the other hand, he felt like a beaten man. As he proudly walked back to his teepee a feeling of hopelessness descended on him. There was nothing he could do now to win her. Moon Beam didn't need him. She would never need him. She had her wolves, and it was obvious she was a very rich woman. He thought long and hard about his situation. His mother was right. He had pushed her out of his life. Now there was not even a glimmer of hope.

Storm thought that Moon Beam might move to the town to have the baby, so he was surprised that she was still living at the cabin as the months rolled by. He found it strange that she was never there when he rode up, even when he approached up very softly.

And then one day, a few months later, everything was out in plain sight inside the cabin. Storm's heart jumped. Moon Beam had stopped hiding things. He felt hope again for the first time in months. Maybe she was starting to forgive him. He had brought fresh meat and dried corn, as he did each time. Unaware of the hidden room in the cabin, he thought she might be short of food because he had never found much of it on the table or in the cupboards. Maybe the wolves killed only when they were hungry, and he wondered if she was surviving the winter on scraps.

Moon Beam thought that was what Storm was thinking when he left fresh meat and dried vegetables each time he visited the cabin. Good, she thought, I won't have to go out hunting with the pack as often. He left other packages too. Storm's mother sent honey, pemmican, bannock, and little baby garments made from soft hides.

Storm worried constantly about her. She had such a small delicate body. Would she be able to give birth without trouble? Moon Beam was huge by the time January was over. She had seen pregnant women at the Indian camp but she couldn't remember anyone being as big as she was. Maybe it was because of her small frame. Sometimes Moon Beam was afraid when she looked down at her enormous belly. She had trouble believe that something as big as a baby could come out of her.

By this time she realized that if Storm came again before the baby was born she would have to face him. She was far too big to run anymore. And it could be dangerous if the baby came early while she was hiding because there was nothing in her hideout to accommodate the birthing of a baby.

Moon Beam had laid out everything she would need: a clean knife to cut the cord, blankets for her and the baby, and clean clothes for her and the child when the birthing was over. She was well prepared. One of the books in her cabin showed pictures of a baby being born step by step and it described what needed to be done once the baby was born. As well, she had the recent advice of the midwife back in Peace River.

Moon Beam's labour began in the middle of February, almost three weeks earlier than she and the midwife had calculated. Shadow paced the cabin, his paws clicking on the wooden floor every time Moon Beam writhed in agony. The contractions began to increase in intensity. Fifteen hours of hard labour passed and still there was no baby. Moon Beam was afraid. Something must be wrong. Why wouldn't the baby come? There was no one to help her and no one to hear her screams. The fire had burned itself out and the cabin grew cold. There was no way she could get up to put more wood on the fire, so it had eventually gone out. Moon Beam wondered if she and the baby, if it were ever born alive, would freeze to death before she had the strength to make another fire. Thoughts of her mother lying on that very same bed kept coming back to her. Who would bury her?

The hours marched by. Moon Beam could not expel the baby from her body, and she got weaker and weaker. The thought that she was going to die long before she ever froze to death was terrifying.

Then, when Moon Beam was hopelessly emerged in a haze of pain, the cabin door opened and Storm walked in. She cried out, "Storm! Help me!" She was not even sure he was real. Was she hallucinating?

Shadow's top lip curled back as deep guttural growls issued from his throat. Storm said, "'Back Shadow! I have to help her." Shadow barked, and hunched himself down to pounce, determined to kill this intruder once and for all. Storm pulled his knife from its sheath as the wolf lunged at him. He got hold of Shadow by the scruff of his neck as the wolf reared up on his hind legs snarling and snapping in Storm's face. Storm raised his other hand with the knife to strike, and stopped mid-air when he heard the whistle. Moon Beam, in a pain-wracked stupor, still had enough wits about her to see what was happening. The wolf dropped to the floor and backed up all the way to the bed, but he watched Storm's every move. Moon Beam spoke softly to her wolf realizing that the poor animal had listened to her screams of pain for days, and was beside himself with fear for her.

"Moon Beam ... how long have you been this way?" Storm asked gently. "I think for two days and nights ... I think this is ... the third day ... She gasped, as another excruciating pain overtook her.

Storm was fearful that something was terribly wrong and hoped it wasn't too late for her and the baby. "Moon Beam, do not worry, I will take care of you." He quickly got a fire going and put the frozen pail of ice on to boil. As soon as there was a little water he washed his hands and walked over to Moon Beam who was now crying softly. Storm sat down on the side of the bed and pulled her into his arms. "Don't cry, Moon Beam, everything is going to be all right now. I want to help you and protect you.

And I'm sorry about everything that has happened between us."

Storm lay her back down and calmly told her that he was going to check her over to see if he could tell why the baby was not coming. Moon Beam was so weak and weary she just nodded her head. She knew that if she was going to make it through this alive, he was her only hope. Once Storm examined Moon Beam it was obvious something was very wrong. He had heard his sisters and his mother talk about difficult and perilous births where the baby comes out bum first. As a young child he had often been present when a baby was born and he had watched, in fascination, everything the women did to help the mother and baby. He drew in his breath and gathered all the courage he could muster. "Moonbeam," Storm said, "the baby is coming the wrong way. I will try to try to turn it to find it's little feet. It is going to hurt you." He talked softly to her the whole time, telling her what he was doing and what was happening, trying to ease her fears. Then he quietly, but urgently, told her she must stop pushing so he could turn the baby.

His hands were shaking as he tried to help the baby, but he simply couldn't turn it. He carefully felt around and finally found the baby's feet and gently pulled them into position. Moon Beam's instinct told her to push and push hard but she held back, groaning in agony. She held on as long as she could and then suddenly, scream after scream came from her as Storm gently pulled the baby out into the world.

The baby made no sound and Storm feared it was

dead. He quickly grabbed a cloth and wiped its face and then put his mouth over the baby's nose and mouth and gave it a few gentle puffs of air. Then, without wasting a second, he turned it upside down and smacked its bottom. The baby gasped its first breath and started to give little mewing sounds that soon turned into a good lusty cry. Storm's heart jumped at the sound and he quickly cut and tied the cord. Grabbing a tiny blanket he wrapped the baby and laid the child next to its mother. Moon Beam smiled weakly and whispered, "What is it Storm, is it a boy or girl?" "I do not know," he grinned sheepishly, as he unwrapped the crying baby to find out. There was silence and then, with a lump in his throat, he whispered reverently, "A girl ... a beautiful little girl."

Now all he had to do was wait for the afterbirth, and if Moon Beam didn't bleed too much everything was going to be just fine. But she suddenly cried out and began groaning again as wave after wave of pain washed over her. Storm, who had just begun to relax, leaped into action with fear in his heart. He could hardly believe his eyes when another little head began to crown. He turned to Moon Beam, who was once more in the throes of pain, and announced, "There is another one!"

Then, about ten minutes later another baby was born, hollering for attention as he entered the cold world. Storm smiled to himself as he cut the cord and wiped the baby's face with warm water. His grin widened as the thought occurred to him that he must have done something right in his life to get two babies at once. "A boy ... it's a boy," he whispered. But the exhausted new mother just smiled and fell into a deep sleep.

Storm covered Moon Beam and the babies with the blanket as he waited for the afterbirth. Then he put some more wood on the fire. The crackling sound of the fire was comforting to him as he looked down at his sleeping family. Once he felt it was warm enough in the cabin, he filled a pan with warm water, and taking one baby at a time, bathed them. Finally, he wrapped the babies securely in little flannel sheets, and then wrapped the hand-knitted woollen blankets around them. Then he laid the babies together and placed them close to Moon Beam's body.

Looking down on them he noticed that their hair was not black like his. Instead, soft blonde fuzz covered their tiny little heads. He couldn't help notice that their skin was a beautiful reddish brown, just like his.

After a few moments of rest, he took a clean warm cloth and gently washed Moon Beams face, neck, and body as she lay sleeping. Then he placed the babies in the cradle and rolled their mother over so he could remove the soiled hides and place clean ones on the bed. Once he was done he put a clean nightgown on Moonbeam and tucked the babies in beside her, covering all three of them with a soft hide he had warmed by the fire. Then, exhausted, he lay down next to her and held her close to him, thanking the Great Spirit for his help in saving Moon Beam and for sending him to her when he did. His last thought as sleep overtook him was that, finally, she had needed him for something.

Storm woke as the light from the windows began to brighten the cabin. He lay there looking at Moon Beam's tired pale face. With all that she had been through, he thought, it was good that the babies slept as long as they did, allowing her to rest. Lying beside her, he realized that it really hadn't been that hard to say he was sorry. In fact, he felt like the weight of the world had been lifted from him. He was feeling free, content, and happy, things he hadn't felt in a long time.

The next week was full as he and Moon Beam got used to looking after the babies. They delighted in sharing their love for the tiny ones. Storm stopped often to stroke Moon Beam's hair or kiss her forehead. He actually laughed at things Moon Beam said, or at the babies when they did something delightful. Simple things such as sucking their mother's breasts for long stretches, then suddenly gasping for air. Even their little cries were a joy.

Storm told Moon Beam that she was a good woman, that he was proud of her, and that it didn't matter if she didn't love him. But Moon Beam felt sadness in her heart whenever he tried to tell her that he cared for her because she really didn't know what she felt for him.

During this time, Shadow was proving to be a real nuisance. He'd scratch to go out, stay out just long enough to do his business and check on his mate, and then he'd scratch to come in again, and hurry back to Moon Beam and the babies. He was completely smitten by the tiny mewling newborns. When they fretted he'd move his head from side to side, whining gently. Moon Beam would often lay the babies down on a moosehide next to the big wolf, letting him keep them warm with the heat of his body. When she had work to do Shadow eagerly looked after the babies. Storm was alarmed the first time he came back into the cabin and saw the babies lying by the wolf, but stopped himself from saying anything.

The babies were two weeks old when Storm asked Moon Beam what she was going to call them. "I'd like to name them Morgan and Brittany, after my parents." And then quickly said, "If that's all right with you." Storm was touched. She had asked him as though she cared about what he thought. Could this be happening? He thought about it and then said, "Those are good Whiteman's names. I would be proud if they have good Indian names too." Moon Beam smiled and said, "What would you like to call them?" Storm told her that he would like to call the little girl Tiny Bird and the boy Little Hawk, after his father. Moon Beam nodded approvingly. She was pleased with his choice of names. And from then on, they were called Tiny Bird Brittany and Little Hawk Morgan.

CHAPTER 17

A Visit From Grandmother and Grandfather

Morning Dew was in a foul mood as she firmly told Flying Hawk, "We are going to where the woman-child lives. Some of the braves know where the place is. My son needs me. We are going." Flying Hawk had used every excuse he could think of to deter her; including telling her she would embarrass her son if they came unannounced. Morning Dew glared at him and repeated that they were going and that he could stay outside in the cold when they arrived, while she went into the dwelling to see the babies and help out.

Flying Hawk gave up. He wondered where Storm got the idea that the man was in control when it came to women and family matters? Not from this family. Too bad he couldn't see his mother now. Let Storm try to tell *her* what to do. It was never going to happen.

By the time Flying Hawk got a few braves together and the horses readied, Morning Dew had everything packed to go. His only job was to pack the horses with the things Morning Dew had set out for him.

Knowing her well, he had readied an extra packhorse. He knew she would bring everything they owned, except the teepee, and even that was a possibility. Flying Hawk was right. She was pleased with him when he didn't complain. He just sighed and packed the horses. She always made him feel good. So, as he expected, when no one was looking she went to his side and gave him a hug, followed by a kiss that could melt river ice. Flying Hawk was pleased that he had given in, as he knew there would be more special attention as soon as they were alone.

It took three days to get to the cabin, as they took their time and enjoyed one another's company. They had camped some distance from the accompanying braves, to allow them privacy to renew their feelings for each other and the attraction they still felt for each other. After all, that's what had brought them together thirty years earlier.

Morning Dew stood watching her husband in the early morning light, as he made ready for the last part of the journey to the cabin. Yes, she said to herself, Storm got his powerful build from Flying Hawk. She was shamelessly watching him steady the horses while he packed them, noticing his rippling back muscles straining against the buckskin on his back. Hawk happened to turn and capture her glance of admiration. As their eyes met, Morning Dew felt herself blushing and, at that same moment, Flying Hawk felt something too.

Hawk stopped what he was doing and, not taking his eyes off his woman, he tied the horse to the tree and walked towards her. Morning Dew was still as beautiful as the day he first laid eyes on her.

It was about noon when they neared the cabin. They could tell they were close when wolves began appearing out of the trees. Morning Dew was afraid. "Storm!" she called out, a little too shrilly, "Are you there?" One of the braves they were travelling with told her that they were very close to the cabin, and that by now Storm knew someone was approaching. Flying Hawk was slightly embarrassed and hoped that his son and the braves would know that he didn't approve of his woman showing fear when he was around to protect her. Morning Dew picked up on this unsaid sentiment and said, "Well Flying Hawk, what will you do if we are attacked by her wolves?" Flying Hawk said quietly, so no one else could hear, "I will ride up to the cabin. If one of the wolves attacks, I will kill it with an arrow."

Inside the cabin Shadow heard the voices first and started to howl. Storm opened the door and followed the wolf out. He was just in time to spot his parents coming down the path. As Shadow started towards them, Flying Hawk swallowed hard. He had seen this big white wolf in the village with Moon Beam, but had always stayed well away from him. Flying Hawk fit an arrow to the bow, just in case. He would have to bring the wolf down before it reached them; because once it was upon them he knew they wouldn't stand a chance. Storm yelled for his father to stop, signalling with his arms as he ran behind the wolf. Shadow stopped and looked back at Storm. Flying Hawk held the arrow fast and Storm heaved a sigh of relief.

Shadow howled and the wolves moved back, disappearing into the bush. But Shadow turned back to the cabin. His instinct told him that Moon Beam was in a weakened state and that his place was beside her. Storm took his parents toward the cabin, explaining on the way what had taken place. Morning Dew cast her dark eyes on Flying Hawk with an I-told-you-so look. It was obvious that Storm was not at all embarrassed. He was happy to see his mother. Morning Dew was convinced they should have come several days ago.

Flying Hawk threw his head back and laughed. What did a father know about mothers and their sons? Storm gave his father a strange look. Of course, he had no idea what was so funny. He wondered for a moment, then shrugged, and hugged his father briefly, as men do. Then he wrapped his arms around his mother for a long meaningful hug.

As they entered the cabin, the big wolf growled until Moon Beam signalled that it was okay. The wolf instantly became quiet, stepped back, and stood beside her. Storm shook his head. He still found it hard to believe the intimate relationship between his woman and the wolf. Now, more than ever before, the wolf wouldn't let Moon Beam out of his sight. From their very first encounter the wolf had picked up on her discomfort with Storm. Even now that they were "friends," Shadow was still leery of him at times. It seemed the wolf wasn't getting over his uneasiness as suddenly as Moon Beam got over hers.

Storm picked up his son and gave him to his grandfather, saying. "Father, this is Little Hawk Morgan." Then he handed him the baby girl for his other arm, "And this is Tiny Bird Brittany." A few minutes later, Moon Beam laughed as she took the baby boy from Flying Hawk's arms and placed him into Morning Dew's arms and then did the same with the baby girl, telling the babies that this was their grandmother. Storm started to frown but then stopped himself and slowly broke into a smile.

Flying Hawk was amazed by the babies and noted that they both looked just like their mother, and exactly like each other. Then Flying Hawk, Morning Dew, Moon Beam, and Storm all laughed as Storm said "*Twins!*" We have twins!"

During the next few days the four of them enjoyed each other's company while doting on the new babies. On the third evening, as they were watching the sun go down Storm said, "Moon Beam, we now have to make some important decisions. What are your plans? Are you going to come to the village with us or are you staying here?" Moon Beam looked at Storm with pain in her eyes. He was not going to understand why she couldn't leave.

She then told him her place was here with the wolves, and that she had bought the land in the valley so the wolves would always be free of interference from men. She explained that she'd bought the land around their village for the same reason, so their people would always have a home. She told Storm that many Whitemen would steal the land and kill both wolves and Indians on sight, that often Whitemen are convinced that they are "civilized" while Indians are not, and that most Whitemen don't understand anyone who is different than they are. It's the same with the wolves. When people don't understand animals they fear them. They have the same fear of each other, because they don't understand each other's ways.

Flying Hawk and Storm stood quietly, nodding their heads. Moon Beam was right. The Whitemen and the Indians did not understand each other. Most of them did not understand the age-old relationship between man and animal. The pelts and hides of the animals fed and clothed people. That is why the Indian people always thanked wolf, fox, bear, caribou, deer, and other animals the for the food and clothing they provided.

Everyone was quiet for a few moments and then Storm said, "You are right Moon Beam. I thank you for the land and the safety of my people. We can never repay you but we promise you that if your wolves wander onto our land, no-one will kill them unless it is means life or death."

Moon Beam thanked Storm and his mother and father for understanding. She then asked Flying Hawk and Morning Dew if she could talk to Storm alone. Once they were alone she asked Storm what his plans were for her and the babies. Storm, as usual, was taken aback by her forthright manner. She always sat him back on his heels with her frankness.

He told her that he wanted her to be his woman, that he cared deeply about her and the babies, and that he wanted to provide for and guide his son and daughter. He told her he wanted to be with her forever and that he hoped someday she would feel the same way about him. Storm told her he would wait and be patient, and that he would never again force himself on her or hurt her. He said, "I want you for my woman. When those Whitemen came to our village I was in pain watching you laughing and talking with them. You did not talk and laugh with me. You were always angry with me."

Astonished, Moon Beam said, "You don't understand. I wish you had asked me instead of becoming so angry with me. Those land surveyors were laughing at me because they didn't believe I could buy the land. They thought no one had that much money, and that I was only a foolish girl. And I was laughing at them because I knew I *did* have enough gold and that they would be very surprised when they found out.

Storm's head snapped back, as he realized that he was an even bigger fool than he had first thought.

He looked so miserable Moon Beam felt sorry for him and softened a little, telling him that he was wrong about her feelings for him and that she would be honoured to be his woman. But, she added, as kindly as she could, she really didn't know if she loved him, and she didn't know much about love either, other than what she had seen of her parents' affection for each other, and from watching the love and affection between her wolves. She said the wolves and the babies needed her too, and asked him if he would be willing to go back and forth between his people and his new family for a while, until she sorted out her feelings.

Moon Beam was beginning to think it would be wonderful if the babies could have a big family of grandparents, aunts and uncles, cousins, friends, and community. It was something she had yearned for through all those lonely years in isolation. She also wanted them to grow up with some schooling, and be able to fit into the Whiteman's world as well as the Redman's.

Storm pointed out that the time for schooling was a long way off and maybe by that time she would feel different. Moon Beam stood close to him in silence, touching his arm while they both looked down at their beautiful babies.

Then Storm gathered his things and the two of them went to his parents, who were patiently waiting outside. They walked over to his horse, with Shadow following behind. As Storm mounted the horse he said to Shadow, "Take care of my woman and babies." Then, pulling his horse around, he looked into Moon Beam's eyes and said, "You will be in my dreams."

CHAPTER 18

Rabies Strikes

The twins were a year old when Moon Beam became pregnant again. Nine months of morning sickness made this pregnancy very hard on Moon Beam. She couldn't understand why this one was so difficult when she had had such an easy time through her first pregnancy. There had been a couple of weeks of feeling sick with the twins, but nothing like this. She hoped there would not be anything wrong with the baby when it was born. And she was worried that it might be malnourished, as she could keep very little down.

Unbelievably, several months later, Moon Beam gave birth to twins again, both girls this time. She and Storm named them together again, Little Brook Sydnee and Little Willow Ashley. But when she entered their names in the Bible she wrote Sydnee Little Brook and Ashley Little Willow. Moon Beam was happy with her little family even though, in her heart, she still didn't know if she loved their father.

It was a hot muggy afternoon and the babies were

cranky, so Moon Beam packed a lunch and took them down to the river to swim. They could have their nap while they were down there. There was no hurry for supper as Storm had gone to the village for a few days. Lounging around at the river was a luxury. As the wolves played, about nine of them were constantly in and out of the river, spraying the babies with their vigorous body shakes. Some of them stopped regularly to lick the babies' faces. The older twins, who were now three, could avoid some of the licking but the babies who were only two had to tolerate the constant face washings. It made Moon Beam laugh. She was happy with her babies, but the minute her thoughts turned to Storm her mood would darken a little.

Moon Beam had brought her bow and arrows with her and while the toddlers were playing she did some target practice. It wasn't often she missed, but as soon as Storm was on her mind she lost concentration. Wind came and lay down beside her, after shaking the fur that was weighing him down. "Wind!" Moon Beam hollered, "Not on me!" She wondered where Shadow was, as she hadn't seen much of him the last few days.

When the babies had had enough swimming and were starting to shiver, Moon Beam hauled them out of the water to rest on a hide she had brought down from the cabin. As they slept, here and there a wolf would lie down and doze in the hot sun. Moon Beam was thinking what a beautiful day it was, when her mind turned again to Storm. In spite of her confused feelings for him, she liked to have him around and often found herself watching him through half-closed eyes (she didn't want him to catch her looking at him). She liked the way he moved. When it was hot and he was half-naked she would admire his broad shoulders and hard muscled chest and stomach.

Moon Beam was often aroused when she watched him like this and when he touched her she would respond immediately. But she hated the feeling of helplessness that overtook her when he made love to her. He told her often how much he cared for her and was always gentle and affectionate, but this just made her sad because she still didn't know whether or not she loved him. Storm was usually quiet after lovemaking and she knew he was waiting for her to express her feelings. But she never did. Something always held her back.

Moon Beam looked over at her sleeping babies and the peaceful scene by the river. Contented, she closed her eyes and went to sleep. She was awakened by Bolt growling, and immediately knew something was wrong. Just then a coyote leaped out of the trees straight at Bolt. The two animals collided in mid-air and it was obvious that neither of them intended to give ground. One of them was going to die. She whistled for the rest of the pack and then gave the command to lay still. Not one of them moved a hair. Never had the pack experienced a situation like this. They all looked at Moon Beam, waiting for her to tell them to help Bolt.

Just then, Shadow walked out of the bush and Moon Beam whistled for him to come to her. He hesitated, but knew he must not disobey the command, so he came close to Moon Beam and watched the battle. The two animals were fighting for their lives, and the coyote was completely crazed. However, it looked like Bolt was getting the best of him. Finally, Bolt had the coyote by the throat. Biting deeply, he began to shake the coyote, and he continued to shake him until he ripped his throat out.

Moon Beam was blinded by tears as she slowly fit an arrow to her bow, "I love you Bolt," she said, as she let the arrow go. The arrow imbedded itself deep in Bolt's heart. He turned, looked at her, and fell to the ground. With a whistle, she ordered the rest of the wolves not to move as she walked over to Bolt and the coyote. "I'm sorry Bolt," she said looking down through tears at her beloved wolf. The pain she felt her made her think she was going to burst wide open. And she did. She moaned and sobbed until nothing more came out of her.

Moon Beam realized that no sane animal would come into a clearing and attack a pack of wolves. She had seen the foaming mouth of the coyote as he came out of the forest in a frenzy. He was rabid, that's why he had attacked. Bolt had been bitten many times, and she knew she had just saved him from weeks of terrible suffering because, with that first bite, Bolt was rabid as well.

Moon Beam whistled, directing the pack to follow her and the children, in order to prevent any of them from getting close to either of the dead animals. As she walked slowly up the hill with the crying children, they met Storm on his way down. She hadn't realized he was back. Storm had never seen Moon Beam lose control of her emotions and he knew something bad had happened. She was nearly hysterical. Words tumbled out of her mouth between gasping sobs, as she asked Storm to help her get the babies to the cabin. She wasn't making much sense but he heard her say something about shooting Bolt with an arrow. When she finally calmed down a bit, she told him a rabid coyote had attacked, and that Bolt had saved them at the cost of his life. Then she stopped suddenly and said, "Shadow will watch over the babies until we burn the bodies. We have to go right now before anything touches them!"

Once the children were safe at the cabin Moon Beam gave the signal for the pack to stay put until she returned. Hurrying back to the dead wolf and the coyote, Storm was shocked to see Bolt with an arrow right through him. No wonder Moon Beam was upset. Storm thanked the Great Spirit for taking Bolt rather than one of the babies. "It is good it is only an animal that lies dead."

Moon Beam stopped dead. Anger overtook her sorrow as she spun around to confront him, "No Storm — he wasn't just an animal — he was my friend!" She continued, in an icy voice. "You can leave. I'll do it myself. I don't want a cold-blooded unfeeling person like you around my wolves or me. You seem to forget that this wolf saved you from the grizzly. And less than an hour ago he fought to his death to protect your children from certain death! He was just as much a part of this family as the children are." At this moment she loathed Storm. She could not believe that he had no understanding of the loss she felt for the beautiful animal that lay at her feet.

Storm knew he had said the wrong thing again and there was no sense trying to make it better. He turned and left. She cursed him under her breath. Storm stopped to go back, and then changed his mind. The little ones needed him more right now more than she did. Apparently, she didn't need anybody other than her wolves, and most of all not him.

Moon Beam set about preparing a fire. After gathering dry deadwood she pushed it all around the wolf and the coyote, constantly aware that she must not to touch them. Then, emotionally exhausted, she lit the fire and watched it consume her beloved wolf, adding more wood from time to time. The smell of burning flesh was repugnant but she kept the fire raging. Many hours later, as the fire burned down, she dug a large hole next to it, and scraped the remains into it to get rid of anything that could spread the disease.

Moon Beam was quiet over the next month, not speaking with to Storm unless absolutely necessary. What was the sense? He was a cold and unfeeling man. During that time, she decided she would never mention Bolt's name to Storm again. She would mourn for Bolt in her own way. This was one of the reasons she had never opened up to Storm. He had told her many times that he cared for her, but somehow she still felt that he didn't understand her.

Day after day, Storm felt her silence, and believed

it would be better if he went back to the village for a while. He hadn't left sooner because he was worried that one of the other animals might be infectious and suddenly attack Moon Beam and the children. It had eased his mind somewhat when they had burned and buried every dead animal they came across. Moon Beam kept her pack close to the cabin, and Shadow even closer. She couldn't bear the thought of her beloved Shadow being rabid. After two or three weeks fewer animals were dying or getting sick. It seemed the disease had run its course. Storm decided it was a good time to go.

A couple of day's later, Storm left for his village to see how the band had made out through the epidemic. Moon Beam felt bitterness and anger towards him when he left. After all, he had always made it quite clear that he thought she could look after herself and the children alone.

When Storm arrived at the village, there was pandemonium. By the time he entered the camp, a group of people had gathered near the trees at the edge of the village. As he started towards them, Flying Hawk rushed out to meet him. His face was white. Storm asked what was happening, as he swung down from his horse. He was worried that something had happened to his mother or his sisters. Flying Hawk said, "It's bad Storm, as bad as it can get. It's Fast Creek" Storm had never seen his strong father lose his composure and it stunned him.

Flying Hawk told Storm that a rabid wolf had bitten his friend. The last few days his condition worsened. He had become so crazed that they'd had to tie him to a tree. Even with four ropes the men could hardly hold him, and now there was nothing more to do but make sure he could not hurt anyone.

Storm walked to the clearing where Fast Creek was tied. Foam leaked from his mouth, and he was bleeding from gashes to his face and body. He had been bashing his head against the tree, and had bitten himself. He was screaming in rage and pain, clawing at himself, and running full speed until he hit the end of the rope. He did this over and over, and then began trying to grab anyone within his reach. Storm could see why his father was so upset. He didn't think the ropes were going to hold Fast Creek for much longer either. The ranting and roaring had already gone on for two days. Flying Hawk couldn't understand how the man could keep going like this without collapsing.

Storm watched Fast Creek for a while. His friend was beyond any human help. There was no recognition in his face for anyone, not even his woman and child. Storm stood and cried for his friend, unashamed of the tears running down his cheeks. He slowly took up his bow and fit an arrow to it. He now understand how Moon Beam felt that day she had to kill her wolf. Storm let the arrow go. It went straight to Fast Creek's heart, and for a fleeting moment he seemed to come back to reality. Their eyes met knowingly a moment before Fast Creek plunged forward into the ropes that held him. In that moment death carried him away.

There were screams of horror when everyone

realized that Storm had shot Fast Creek, then silence as the shock set in. Quiet hung over the village for some time. Gone were the bloodcurdling screams of his trusted friend. Only sobs were heard in the stillness as the people mourned for one of their own. Storm had saved his friend from two or three more days of agonizing pain and hopeless frenzy.

Storm's shoulders shook with his sobs. Sometimes it was hard to be a chief. When he regained his composure he quietly told the men to bring firewood. If the people were in shock over Storm shooting Fast Creek, they were going to be even more upset when they realized that the chief was going to burn Fast Creek's body immediately, giving them no time to wash it, no time to properly prepare him on his way to the Great Spirit. No time to say goodbye. Some of the men hesitated when they realized what Storm was going to do, but it wasn't long before there were stacks of wood around the tree. Storm lit the wood and watched for many hours as the men continued to feed the fire long into the night. The flames gradually consumed Fast Creek's body until there were only ashes and bones left. The men then dug a hole and scraped the remains into it.

Storm asked the villagers if Fast Creek had touched anyone else in the last week or two. It was possible he'd had physical contact with his woman and child, so Storm immediately went to Fast Creek's lodge to find them. Fast Creek's woman was crying softly and holding her whimpering child. Storm asked her if Fast Creek had touched her. Little Owl told him that when

Fast Creek had come home her monthly time was upon her and nothing had happened between them. Then Little Owl looked at Storm and said with trepidation, "He played with the baby and kissed her. He held and kissed me also ... Oh no Storm! ... No ... You don't think we have the biting sickness do you?"

"I do not know Little Owl but we will have to keep you and the baby away from the rest of the tribe. Do not touch anyone. You can keep the baby with you. If she does not have the sickness yet, you may have passed it on to her through your milk. Little Owl wept with the fear her child might have to die. As she held her baby close, she decided that if they had to die they would die together.

By the time Storm turned and left Little Owl clinging desperately to her child, the people had returned to their dwellings to mourn the loss of Fast Creek. He had been greatly admired and much loved by the people and now a terrible twist of fate had taken him away.

Morning Dew came forward to meet her son. She had seen everything, not only what happened in the days leading up to this tragedy, but also Storm's execution of Fast Creek. She opened her arms and her big strong son walked into them and put his head down on hers.

Flying Hawk wished that he to could go to his son and comfort him as Morning Dew was doing, but he worried it would embarrass Storm. He started to walk away, then thought better of it. His woman never worried that she might embarrass the boy. Why did he think he would embarrass his son by showing emotion? Turning back toward them, he walked back to his son and put his arm tightly around his shoulder, and gently said, "That was a hard thing to do. I do not know if I could have done it." Storm leaned for a few seconds against his father, trying to suck some of his strength into his own depleted body.

Storm stayed a month with his people. He knew they needed him in this time of sorrow and fear. Although he worried about his own family, he knew the wolves were there to protect them. He also knew he had to stay until he was sure that Little Owl and her baby were going to be all right. He visited them every day, watching, worrying, and observing the mother's and the child's physical and mental state. He had hardly slept since Little Owl had told him that if she and the baby got sick he was the one who must kill them. He was sick at heart but he knew he mustn't show his weakness to her. He kept his emotions hidden and simply nodded his head, saying, "If you get sick, I will ask Flying Hawk to help me and you and your baby will die at the same moment." As the days turned into weeks it became obvious that Little Owl and her baby had not been infected.

CHAPTER 19

The Aftermath

Moon Beam had her hands full with the children and with sewing clothes as fast as she could. The babies were growing so fast she felt she just couldn't keep up. There simply wasn't enough of her to go around. On the one hand, she was angry at Storm for having been gone so long. On the other, she was more than a little concerned and hoped everything was all right in the village. But she was also quite sure that if Storm were in trouble someone would come and tell her.

It was dusk when Moon Beam heard hooves pounding up to the cabin. She hurried to the door and saw that it was Black. When he saw her he gave a scream that sent chills down her back. He was lathered and breathing hard. She knew something was very wrong back at Black's herd. Moon Beam called Salt and Pepper to her, telling them to stay with the little ones. She put bread and water and small pieces of meat out for the babies, warning the wolves to leave the children's food alone. She also told them to keep the little ones inside the cabin and not let them play in the fireplace, which was out but full of cold ashes. The wolves whined at her but one lay down in front of the fireplace and the other placed itself across the open doorway.

Moon Beam grabbed her gun and put it over her shoulder, slipping her large knife in the belt around her waist. She kissed the children goodbye, told the wolves once again to look after the babies, and ran outside to Black. Grabbing his mane she swung up on his back. He was in a full run before she was even settled. Moon Beam grimaced, recalling that she had taken many a tumble off Black before she had learned to ride with the skill she now had. She whistled for the wolves. Shadow, along with his mate Fawn and the rest of the pack, emerged here and there from the trees to run alongside. Moon Beam noticed that Shadow and Black, for some reason, were letting the rest of the pack run close to them. In all the years she had known these animals, she had never seen Shadow or the horse allow the pack to come in that close. Moon Beam knew the pack sensed Black was in trouble and that it was something he couldn't handle alone. Somehow the wolves knew the horse needed them and wanted them close.

Black's herd was about five miles out in a clearing, which was unusual. He had never brought his herd in this close. As they neared the herd Moon Beam was close to tears. Black had a rabid mare in his midst and didn't know what to do. He had chased her back repeatedly while trying to push the rest of the herd towards

Moon Beam and the cabin. The last two days had been the worst, as the mare had gotten close enough to kill three foals. Stomping and biting, she had dragged them around until they were completely still. Each time the other mares went back to fight for their foals, Black stopped them. Somehow he sensed that he had to keep the herd away from the rabid mare.

As Moon Beam overlooked the bedlam, she signalled some of the wolves to go in close, hoping the mare would chase after them. Other wolves were sent in to herd the horses towards her. Once the wolves had separated the mare from the herd, she raised her rifle, aimed, and pulled the trigger. The sick mare, which was galloping full speed toward the wolves, went head over heels as the bullet found its mark. The dust settled around the infected mare as she died. Both her suffering and her rampage were over.

Moon Beam whistled for the wolves to stay back from the dead horse. Then she signalled them to herd the rest of the horses and colts back to Black. Moon Beam swung down from the horse and checked him over from top to bottom, including inside his mouth. He was one lucky stallion. She was astounded that he hadn't been bitten by the mare with all the fighting that been going on.

After she recovered for a few moments, she stood carefully observing the mares and foals. Suddenly, she felt her stomach go into knots as she spotted a mare with a bite on her back. Moon Beam raised her gun and fired and the mare dropped like a stone. She watched as the mare's foal ran to its dead mother. She fired again, and then continued to look over the herd, trying not to think about what had to be done next. By the time she was finished she had spotted four more bitten foals and had to shoot them too. Black was beside himself and didn't understand what was happening. Why was Moon Beam killing the herd? Black seemed to know that the first mare had to die but couldn't make the connection as to why seemingly healthy horses had to die too. "I'm sorry Black," Moon Beam said more to herself than the horse, "but they've been bitten by the sick mare and it's only a matter of time before they're as crazy and sick as she was."

Moon Beam was a long time burning and burying the mares and seven dead foals. She was worried about her little ones back at the cabin. It had been over twenty-four hours since she had left them. When she was finally done she called Black, whistled for the pack, and said, "Take me home to my babies Black." As soon as she mounted the horse she collapsed onto his mane in exhaustion and held on tight.

When they arrived back at the cabin the youngest babies were sleeping peacefully beside Salt on the hide in front of the fireplace. The other twins had gotten into the flour bin and had spread flour all over the floor. They were having a great time rolling around in it with Pepper.

Moon Beam had to laugh at the big wolf, "You're a baby watcher, but I guess this is what you get when you leave wolves to do the job." Then she set about washing her body and her clothes to make sure she hadn't brought the disease home to her family. Once the cabin was tidied and the children tucked in bed Moon Beam laid her tired quivering body down. She didn't think she could take much more of this rabies ordeal. Would it be over before it got to her other wolves or her children? Or would it never stop?

When Storm arrived back home, he was very quiet and sad. He greeted the children warmly and seemed more glad than usual to see them. Moon Beam put the children to bed early then went to her husband. She was surprised to realize she had missed him. Taking his head in her hands she pulled his head to her breast, asking him softly what was wrong. Her usually imperious husband whispered, "I had to shoot Fast Creek." Moon Beam's heart jumped so hard she thought it was going to explode out of her chest. She held him tight as he told her what had taken place back at his village. The horror of what had taken place would be a long time passing for both of them, but Moon Beam knew that time would heal. Someday, the realization that he'd had no choice would lessen the pain.

Moon Beam felt truly sorry for this very brave man ... her man. He would always have to make difficult decisions for his people, and not all of these would make him a hero. For the first time a feeling of tenderness washed over Moon Beam for him. And this time she didn't try to push that feeling away as she had always done in the past. Maybe she was learning to understand Storm, and maybe, just maybe, she was beginning to care about him.

Months went by and the rabies ran its course

and died out. The wolves were let out to roam again. Moon Beam had lost seventeen wolves, four mares, and seven foals to this insidious disease. Moon Beam and Storm each grieved in their own way for the ones they had loved and lost. And both of them gained a new respect for each other.

CHAPTER 20

Life is Good ... Except ...

Time passed and peace reigned in the valley. Moon Beam was grateful for the quiet and solitude. She spent more quality time with her children now and was enjoying every minute of being a mother, rather than worrying about how difficult it could be. As the children got bigger she began taking them with her when she went out with the wolves. The wolves gave the children lessons in survival, nipping and nudging them when they got to close to a cliff or deep running water. If one of them fell into the water, the wolves would haul the child out. They seem to know that the little humans didn't know how to swim, even though their own pups knew how to swim as soon as they were big enough to go into water.

Moon Beam did not interfere when the wolves guided and protected her children. They had to learn the ways of the wild and their place in the scheme of things. They also had to learn which wolves were more tolerant in the pack. It didn't take them long to know to stick close to Shadow and some of the older wolves. The young wolves hadn't yet learned patience and didn't easily tolerate their ears and eyes being poked. The pups, on the other hand, were usually in just as much trouble as the little humans were, so they were great company.

Storm often went back and forth between the village and the cabin. For the most part this was fine with Moon Beam. He was good to the children and occasionally took the older twins with him to visit their grandparents, sometimes staying away for a couple of weeks. Moon Beam was content when he was gone, not because she didn't miss him, but because she often felt as if they were on the verge of an emotional impasse. She knew Storm needed something more from her but, she still felt he was fighting her on some level, at least where the wolves and a couple of other issues were concerned. So, once more, she closed her heart to him. She had made up her mind that if he didn't want the same things in life as she did, then he was just wasting her time.

Moon Beam was beginning to think that she had given Storm more support than he ever gave her. His village and his people always seemed to come first, and he'd leave her alone for weeks on end to contend with rearing of their children. She couldn't go to his village, because the wolves would have to come with her, and dogs and wolves just don't mix. Time and time again he left, saddling her with the responsibility of protecting them and providing food, water, and firewood. Besides, Moon Beam resented the fact that

Storm relied on the wolves to help provide her with meat. And she convinced herself that the wolves were more responsible than he was in providing for them.

It seemed to her that Storm still needed to be the dominant one in the relationship. It was his way or no way. And, thinking about this, she concluded that Storm did not treat the children equally. He favoured his son over his daughters. Moon Beam would try to explain to him that the girls were as capable of learning to do things as the boy was. Storm did not like it when Moon Beam taught the girls to ride Black. He didn't like it when Moon Beam took them hunting with her and the wolves. It was okay for Little Flying Hawk to go hunting, because Storm believed that would be the boy's role in life. "Why do you want to teach the girls the ways of men?" he would ask.

This stubborn man didn't give in easily and it usually took a lot of heated discussion before he finally gave in. This angered her, especially when he'd say, "You want our daughters to be like you." Then Moon Beam would fight back the tears, not allowing him to see the hurt he inflicted with his thoughtless words.

Storm knew his words were hurtful at times and he often felt sorry afterwards. And deep down he knew that most of his bitterness stemmed from her independence. He felt she didn't need him and, he admitted to himself on more than one occasion, he was jealous of the wolves. He tried to curb his feelings but it never seemed to happen before he'd hurt his woman with his words.

Moon Beam continued to keep her distance from

him emotionally and physically. If she was that inadequate as a woman and if he was so worried that the girls would turn out like her, then why did he want her to be his woman? He came to visit the children whenever it pleased him, and she never kept him from taking the children to visit their grandparents.

Even taking the children to the village would result in a showdown because, more frequently than not, Storm would take his son and leave the girls behind. He claimed it was good for the boy because, one day, Little Flying Hawk would be chief and had a lot to learn. The girls, on the other hand, would only have cooking, cleaning, planting, and the care of the family to do. Try as she might, Moon Beam just couldn't get through to him that he was hurting the girls and alienating them from him.

Moon Beam's feelings of hopelessness and her belief that she could never please him sometimes had her wishing he would go away one day and never come back. Maybe they would never understand each other.

CHAPTER 21

A Psychopathic Stalker

Something wasn't right in the wolf world, but Moon Beam couldn't put her finger on the problem. Some of the wolves seemed spooked and this made her uneasy as well. She had a feeling that she was being watched and, at times, stalked. Moon Beam had been sending the wolves out on patrol around the cabin or ahead of her and the children when they went on an outing. At first she thought it had to be her imagination, because she knew nothing could get close to her without the wolves giving her a warning. However, when her wolves started disappearing she became really concerned.

Moon Beam searched for the missing wolves and sometimes found their carcasses stashed or buried as though someone were hiding them. She had never been so distraught. Somehow she had to stop the carnage. Whoever or whatever was doing this wasn't killing for fur or meat. They were killing her beautiful animals. Time after time the wolves would lead her to dead animals or to camps where someone had taken great pains to cover their tracks and erase evidence of the camp. It looked to Moon Beam like the wolves were being lured by fresh meat while tracking the killer, and she surmised that once the wolves got too close they were killed before they could go back to warn Moon Beam.

Someone out there was outwitting her wolves and killing them to keep them from coming to her. Someone was stalking her. But why? She became much more cautious, and no longer ventured far from the cabin. Aside from the times the wolves went hunting in relays, she kept them close to the cabin to protect her and the little ones.

Moon Beam found herself wishing Storm were around more, that he would be home just once when she needed him. Nevertheless, she was managing on her own, until Shadow disappeared. Then the search began in earnest. Each day she would move her children to safety, and then set out to kill whatever was killing her wolf family. The cold calculating animal instinct entered the woman who was, after all, half-human and half-wolf. Another human would not have recognized the wolf-woman standing there in the wilderness.

Many times over the years, she'd had to become part wolf to survive. Consequently, as an adult, she did not hesitate to kill. She was determined that the only place the killer of her wolves was going was straight to hell.

Moon Beam decided drastic measures were

needed. So, accompanied by six wolves, she set out on Black with the children riding on the travois behind. The wolves remained out of sight but close behind, as she headed Black towards the Indian village. They left in the dark of the night so they could not easily be followed. Once she was a couple of hours away from the village she took the older children down from the horse, and told Morgan and Brittany they had to hold onto the little twins' hands at all times. She gave them food and water and told them to go to their father. Then she instructed the wolves to stay with them until they were safe with Storm.

Moon Beam was worried but assured herself they would be fine the rest of the way with the wolves. The children were now four and five years of age. Having been reared in the wilderness with a pack of wolves they weren't at all afraid and were quite capable. Pepper had been to the village several times and she knew he would protect the children until his last breath. She signalled three wolves to take one side of the children and two to take the other. Pepper was told to stay out in front of the children. Moon Beam knew that he would not let them out of the middle of his small pack under any circumstances. Besides, Little Flying Hawk had made the trip many times with his Father, and he knew the way as well.

Moon Beam kissed them all goodbye and watched them until they were out of sight. Then she mounted Black and pressed him hard in the side with her knees. The horse, feeling her urgency, bunched his muscles and ran as hard as he could. Moon Beam's main concern now was whether or not Shadow was still alive and how the killer had tricked her wolf. Shadow was smart, smarter than a lot of humans were, so how did he get caught?

Meanwhile, Shadow had been on the trail of something that smelled like fresh blood or meat for a couple of days. He was wily enough to know it wasn't an animal he was tracking but something that walked on two legs, something evil and sinister. His inborn sense told him that if he weren't careful it would kill him. He knew that whatever he was hunting was hunting him. Whatever it was would at times circle Shadow from behind and follow him until Shadow sensed it was near. Then Shadow would lose the stalker in a creek.

The third day out the stalker captured Shadow. The wolf had known that whatever was tracking him was pushing him from behind. Shadow followed the same routine and headed for the creek to lose the hunter. Suddenly, the earth gave out beneath his paws and he plunged down into a deep pit. Winded, the big wolf was still trying to catch his breath when a head came into view over the side of the pit. The man looked down at the wolf, which continued to lie very still with his eyes half-closed watching the human. Pure instinct made the wolf lay quiet. Even one flick of his tail and the man at the top would shoot him. He heard the man laugh, "Thought you were smarter than me, you son of a bitch, but you got a broken neck out of it didn't you?" Then he turned and walked away from the pit, thoroughly relaxed. With the lead wolf gone, the girl was his for the taking.

And once he got her he was going to force her to show him where she had found the gold. He had waited five years for her to return to the town with more gold, but she hadn't and he couldn't wait any longer. There had to be more of the gold. The girl could only have found that many nuggets if there were more lying about.

He had been tracking her for days. He did wonder where those kids had come from because she hadn't had any when she had come to town with the gold. He had been planning this for a long time. It had been easy to get the sheriff to talk because Sheriff John trusted him. There was nothing to point any suspicion his way either, after he made Moon Beam disappear that is. He knew all about the wolves. John had excitedly told him about the big white wolf and his devotion to the girl. He knew if he got the big wolf and a few others out of the way he could handle the girl.

Grinning sadistically he headed to the cabin. Whatever wolves were in his way now he would just shoot. Nothing was going to stop him. Finding the valley hadn't been hard. He just followed the map in his office. Good-hearted easy-going Nels had fooled a lot of people over the years. Many had trusted him and several of those were dead. Nels was already a wealthy man, but he had managed to hide the real reason he killed miners and trappers, and that was the sheer thrill of killing.

Occasionally, the sheriff and Nels met with a

miner or trapper who was doing well, John sometimes
had a funny feeling about Nels, but he usually pushed
it away. Unfortunately, human nature compelled
these unfortunate souls to brag about their mining
claims or about how much money they had made
trapping. John always thought it was a little odd that,
a year or so later, these newly rich men disappeared.
Just dropped out of sight and were never seen again.
Sometimes other trappers or miners would find a
corpse and bring it out of the bush, but most of the
time only scattered bones told of their demise. Other
times it was families who were looking for missing
relatives. At times John thought he had an epidemic
on his hands as he looked for missing people, but
when he found no bodies or evidence of foul play,
he figured the people had just moved on. But one
thing, almost consciously, nagged him. Once in a
while when a body was found and recognized, John
would remember meeting the man with Nels present,
because they had to go to his office to file a claim.

Nels always knew who struck it rich and who
didn't. And John had recently begun to notice that
the men who weren't rich stayed alive. Nels made
a lot of trips to Edmonton and John just presumed
he was going on business. Little did he know that
on many of these trips Nels never even left the area.
He was sometimes gone for up to a month, but for
the most part it was a week or less. Eventually, John
became suspicious whenever somebody disappeared
around the same time that Nels did. He had recently
begun to follow Nels. On two occasions Nels had not

gone anywhere near the big city, but had taken the stagecoach to another town then back-tracked home stopping at places close to new mining areas.

John was looking at Nels through different eyes now, but as yet he had no evidence that any crimes had been committed. This time John had followed Nels to Moon Beam's valley, which he recognized from the maps Moon Beam had left with him. John was pretty sure her wolves protected the girl well enough if Nels was out to hurt her in any way, but then he began finding dead wolves. And then he got really worried.

John was careful not to reveal himself, but it didn't take Nels long to realize he was being tracked. He caught up with John and stealthily attacked him from behind. John didn't even know what hit him. When he regained consciousness a couple of days later he was lying at the bottom of a steep riverbank. He didn't know by what grace of God he'd landed on the riverbank and not in the river. He'd have been swept away by the current and that would have been the end of him.

Nels hadn't shot or knifed the sheriff because he didn't want any marks on the body that would indicate murder. If John's corpse were ever found, Nels wanted it to look like the man had been thrown from his horse.

After he got his wits about him, John crawled to the water and washed his face. His nose was broken and his head smashed by the butt of a rifle but, amazingly, he had no broken bones. He hurt everywhere from the beating and the fall and he figured if his skull wasn't fractured he'd live to fight another day. John didn't dare call for help at the bottom of the bank in case Nels realized he wasn't dead and came back to finish him off. All he could hope for was that maybe Moon Beam's big wolf would find him.

Rachel made it back to the cabin the following morning. After a brief rest she called for the wolf pack and sent most of them out to look for Shadow. By this time, Nels was getting frustrated. Every time he got close to her there were too many wolves around her. He had figured he'd be able to grab her at the cabin, but she never stayed there for more than a few minutes. However, she regularly sent wolves back there to check to see if Shadow had returned.

Back at the village, Storm was overcome with shock when six wolves and four small children wandered into the village without their mother. He could only get bits of information from them, but they were quite clear that Shadow, the mighty wolf, was lost. Storm immediately sent the wolves from the camp before the village dogs descended on them. He lost no time in taking the children to their grandmother. Within fifteen minutes he was riding at a full gallop, headed for the cabin, with the six wolves by his side.

Shadow lay in the darkness of the pit until everything was quiet. Then he tried jumping at the sides of the pit in an effort to get out. Over and over he tried until he was exhausted. He dared not howl for the other wolves because the human would come back and kill him.

By this time, John had recovered enough to start crawling along the riverbank. Somehow he had to find a way up so that he could get help for Rachel. Unknown to him, his situation was the same as that of the trapped wolf. Neither of them could call for help because of the risk that the killer would come back to finish them off.

John was appalled that he'd been so naïve and unsuspecting about Nels for all those years. He had talked about the missing people. He'd told Nels where he had looked and where he was going to search next. He had even told him where the miners had hidden their gold or where the trappers said they'd hidden the cash they accumulated from trapping. John believed he was just as guilty of the murders as Nels was. He had set these men up for the taking and nobody had been the wiser.

After hours of searching, John finally found a way up the cliff. Clawing his way to the top on his hands and knees, he finally made it over the top. He soon found some a creek and was surprised at how thirsty he was and how cool and refreshing the water was. John lay there and rested for a couple of hours before pushing himself to his feet. Still exhausted, he staggered around, wandering through the bush wherever he thought he could see the traces of a trail. He hadn't gone far when he came to a huge hole in the ground. In fact, he had narrowly missed stumbling into it. That's all I need, he thought. He fell to his knees and crawled to the edge of the hole to look down. There at the bottom was Rachel's big white wolf. John

gasped, whispering, "Shadow ... is that you boy?"
He'd been hoping to find one of the wolves, but not
at the bottom of a pit. "Nel's dirty work again," John
muttered in disgust.

Shadow knew that he had heard John's voice before
and that Rachel had introduced him to this man. He
knew John was no threat, so he whined gently telling
the man he needed help. "Hang on boy! John said, "I'll
figure out a way to get you out of there." He found a
few half-rotten logs and pushed them down into the
pit. He realized they weren't long enough, but if the
wolf got up high enough he might be able to jump the
rest of the way. Sure enough, the logs were just high
enough so that Shadow could leap up and out. He
walked over to the man and sniffed him.

John recalled Moon Beam saying that the wolf
would remember his scent after being introduced to
it, and that John would be able to trust the wolf with
his life if they should ever meet again. John noticed
Shadow was limping on his back leg and thought it
might be broken. But the wolf wasn't letting this slow
him down much. He turned and went back towards
the creek for a long drink of water. John had no way
of knowing that the wolf had been in the hole a day
longer than he'd been at the bottom of the cliff. Four
days had left Shadow hungry, thirsty, and very weak.
John patiently waited and then followed the wolf,
stopping wherever the animal stopped. When the wolf
went onto his belly and started to slither silently on
the ground so did John. Shadow was stalking food and

John, having no weapon, knew that he was dependant on the wolf to provide him with food as well.

Sure enough, it wasn't long before the wolf had something big. Leaping and snarling Shadow pulled the deer down and it didn't take long for the thrashing animal to die. John crawled through the tall grass and there was Shadow standing over the deer. The little doe hadn't had much of a chance against the big wolf. Of course, he had to wait until the wolf had taken his fill as Shadow bared his teeth when the man looked at him, and John instantly got the message.

And that's the way Storm found them both ... eating blood-dripping meat. They were dirty and dripping blood themselves but they were alive. John grabbed for a chunk of wood to defend himself from this huge frightening Indian. Storm's eyes narrowed at the man's actions, then looked at the wolf and addressed him instead. "Shadow, where is Moon Beam?" Storm said. The wolf immediately threw his head back and howled. Storm turned to the man and demanded, "Who are you and what are you doing with this wolf?" John replied," I'm Rachel's Uncle John. I followed a man here who's out to hurt her. And who are you?" John asked, knowing he must be a friend of the wolf. "I am Storm, chief of my village and Moon Beam, the woman you call Rachel, is my woman."

"What happened here?" asked Storm. John explained the best he could about Nels and about how everyone in and around Peace River had trusted the man. He told Storm that he had set out to track Nels down when he finally realized the man was a cold-blooded murderer.

John then explained how he had found himself at the bottom of the cliff, how he'd painstakingly climbed the bank and wandered around until he stumbled on the wolf by almost falling in the hole.

Storm asked if they had seen Moon Beam. He explained that he had left his village after his children had arrived with the wolves, and that he grew concerned when Shadow was nowhere around. He trusted Shadow, as the wolf was always at Moon Beam's side, and he told John that he'd had a strong feeling that something was terribly wrong. He'd suspected that Moon Beam had sent her young brood with the other wolves because something had happened and they were in danger. He'd come to the conclusion that Shadow had disappeared and Moon Beam was out searching for him.

Storm helped John up on his horse and led the animal through the dense bush towards the cabin. He planned to start from there to track his Moon Beam. He knew she had the rest of the pack with her and that she'd be fairly safe from the killer if her wolves surrounded her.

Storm didn't let on, but he was ashamed. He had put the responsibility on a wolf to look after his family. He had taken the easy way out in dealing with Moon Beam's frustration and anger. He'd simply gone back to his tribe every time she became difficult. As he thought back, it struck him that he hadn't been back to the cabin since the rabies attack on one of her beloved wolves. Through the whole epidemic he'd never been there when his family was under attack.

But Shadow had been. No wonder she loved that wolf. And no wonder Moon Beam was often withdrawn and cool towards him. How could she rely on him when he was never there for her? It must have left her wondering how he could be gone for weeks, then suddenly show up and start telling her how she and their children should live their lives.

Worse yet, he had done this over and over. No wonder the mother of his children was always so angry towards him. He knew now, that he should have stayed when she pushed him away, telling him to go back to his village. He had acted like a woman and obeyed. Never again. If he were lucky enough to find her alive he would act like a man from now on. He would protect his family.

As worried as Storm was he grinned to himself. This man, Nels, does not know what he is dealing with. He does not know that the easygoing little waif he met back in town is not the same one he is going to deal with out here. If he thinks Moon Beam is going to be easy to capture, he is in for a big surprise.

"What do you think Nels wants?" Storm asked John. "Gold," John said quietly, "He knew Rachel ... I mean Moon Beam ... had taken gold to town and he thought there must be more. Once he catches her and finds out where she's hidden the gold, he'll kill her." Storm told John he did not think that was going to happen, that somebody was going to die but it was not going to be Moon Beam. John looked quizzically at Storm, wondering what the Indian was talking about.

But he hoped they would find her before Nels did, because he now knew just how twisted this man was.

Nels, being Nels, and never having been caught in anything he did, was feeling pretty cocky. He grinned like the lunatic he was at the thought of how he would make her talk. Hell, she'd be nothing to grab after getting rid of the big white wolf and good old John. He'd caught sight of her tracks and was pretty damn sure that because she was with the wolves she wouldn't bother hiding her tracks. He knew that once he'd killed a few more of her wolves and had his hands on her, she'd try to send the wolves away so he couldn't hurt them. But his plan was to just keep shooting anything in his way. And she wouldn't be able to stand the sight of dead wolves everywhere.

Moon Beam stood on a knoll behind a tree watching the man's actions. He'd shot another two wolves just because they were there. Moon Beam kept calling to the wolves in their own language. No one could tell the difference between her call and the pack's. The hunter had now become the hunted. She was warning the wolves to stay hidden and under no circumstances to show themselves unless she called for them. Moon Beam kept leading the man around in circles, having already figured out that this fool thought that she was a naive terrified girl. Soon, Moon Beam would let him catch a glimpse of her, now that the trap had been set. Moon Beam didn't know who the man was yet and she didn't know where Shadow was — but she knew for sure that this man was a born killer.

Shadow had never been away from her this long. Moon Beam was thinking that if he hadn't heard her howls and come to her by this time, he might be dead. Every time Moon Beam visualized Shadow dead, an overwhelming anger rose up inside her. This man was going to pay dearly for killing her wolves.

Moon Beam walked out into the open and waited for the man to see her, pretending she was not aware of his presence. When she was sure he had seen her she vanished into the trees.

Nels, spotting her, gave chase. The stupid bitch was almost his. He caught sight of Moon Beam at a distance, crossing a log over a deep ravine. It was the only way across and he continued to follow her. Halfway over he stopped cold. Moon Beam was standing there on the other side smiling at him. But the smile didn't match the cold calculating look in her eyes as she recognized him. "Hello Nels," she said sweetly, "Fancy meeting you here." Standing beside her stood three huge wolves. With a hand signal from Moon Beam the wolves started to cross the log towards him. He was raising his rifle to shoot the wolves when something bumped him from behind. Twirling around, he was confronted by a large pure white wolf. At first, he thought it was the big white male but then realized this one was smaller. Behind the white wolf were five or six more. Startled, he stepped sideways — bad move. Losing his balance he went off the side of the log and plunged into the ravine. The last thing he saw was the icy fixed smile on Moon Beam's face.

When Nels came to he was hanging upside down

from a tree, his hands free but not able to touch the ground. Moon Beam was leaning against another tree still smiling strangely at him. " Nels," she said, "Could you tell me what you might have done to a big white wolf?" Something in her quiet and unemotional voice made him shudder ... and that look in her eyes ... it was completely unnerving. He fought a gagging dryness in his throat and finally managed to croak, "I saw a big white wolf ... I ... I ... saw him fall into a deep hole." Moon Beam nodded and said nothing for a moment or two then she asked him in a deadly calm voice, "What are you doing in these parts? And why are you killing my wolves?"

Nels couldn't think, he was dizzy and fighting the urge to empty the contents of both his stomach and his bowels. He made a feeble but desperate attempt at lying, and croaked out, half-gagging on his own words, "Uh ...uh ... I ... I ... just passing through ... told you I'd look you up... if I ... uh ... passed this way ... didn't shoot your wolves ... not me ... someone ... else." Moon Beam waited patiently, nodding and smiling, then said icily, "Oh yes you did, you killed my wolves and you've been stalking me." Silence followed. Then Nels croaked, "Not me. I just got here ... yesterday." Moon Beam nodded again.

He could see that she that was fiddling with something in her hands but he couldn't make out what she had. As she approached the tree he was hanging from she said, "Did you know there's a name in the wild for sick creatures like you? ... They're called "rogue" animals. They kill just for the sake of killing." Silence.

He could barely breathe. "So ... the wolves and I are going to let you meet a rogue ... a true monster just like you." As she spoke she cut the neck of the rabbit she was holding with her big knife, letting the blood splash all over Nels. Once the rabbit was bled out she careful placed it between his legs, and said, "You know, I have a feeling that isn't what you thought was going to be between your legs if you had gotten hold of me." Moon Beam turned and whistled for the pack to follow. Nels swore and screamed foul names at her, and then suddenly there was silence again.

A sudden horror had crept into his consciousness as it dawned on him what was about to happen to him. She was going to leave him dangling upside down from a tree with a decapitated rabbit between his legs. He was a dead man. He didn't know how he was going to die but it was certain his hours on earth were numbered.

Well, he thought, one thing for sure ... if he was going to die he was going to make her life hell. He hollered at her retreating back. "I killed your wolf, bitch! He's in a deep hole with a broken neck and you'll find your Uncle John at the bottom of the river!"

Moon Beam flinched. She wanted to go back to him and plunge her knife into him again and again until he was dead. But her wolves knew what punishment lay in store for this man. He was going to die a horrible death. He was going to have time to be really terrified. Maybe he'd think about the wolves that lay dead in his wake. Moon Beam knew, intuitively, that if he had killed her Uncle John, it wouldn't have been the first man this demented bastard had killed. But it sure was going to be the last.

Dusk was falling before Nels had any inkling of what was to come. Then, he heard the low grunts of the grizzly before it came into view. Even in the outside world, word had gotten around about the rogue grizzly that was terrorizing the country. There had been many horrifying stories about the bear that packed kids right out of their yards, and of mothers he had killed while they tried to protect their children. This grizzly was known to break the doors of cabins down to get in, and it always seemed he attacked when the man wasn't home. The crazed grizzly had killed farm animals by the dozen, not even eating them. *He killed because he loved to kill.* A "rogue" ... this was Nels' last thought as the bear attacked.

Moon Beam, who was about a half-a-mile away, heard the screaming in the distance. Sound carries very well in the quiet of the evening. As she headed away from the screams she didn't want to miss one piercing scream. It was a balm to her wolf soul. As the screams reached a hideous pitch wolves across the valley joined other howlers of the wild in the mass hysteria. Moon Beam threw her head back and joined in. The howls that came from her throat, and from her very being, were the mourning cries of a wolf when one of their own dies. This was the only way she knew to mourn the loss of Shadow.

Storm and John heard the screams about a mile away. Shadow flew past them once he heard the howling of the others. He feared he was about to be separated once and for all from the girl he loved. No wolf or human knew that mourning call better than Shadow.

As the wolf thundered on toward the howls it seemed the whole night came alive. The coyotes, not to be outdone, began to howl along with the wolves. Even the loons took up the lonely call. Only when a great leader in the wild dies does the whole of nature join in the death cry. And Shadow sensed the cries were for Moon Beam. The animals of the night knew something evil had died, but they also knew that the grizzly was still a threat to them all. One of them had to kill him.

Shadow stopped after a while, just long enough to join in the mourning howls. Moon Beam instantly recognized his howls, even before he came into sight, and she started running towards the sound just as Shadow came bounding out of the trees. The wolf slowed considerably but knocked her down anyway, as he threw his body into her arms. Moon Beam clasped her arms around him and held him tight, sobbing relentlessly into his neck.

A few minutes later Storm and John came into view. Storm helped John, who was still very weak, off the horse, then stood, looking his woman over. There were no marks but she still had the look of the hunter on her and Storm knew she had made a clean kill.

Storm, being careful not to be seen or smelled, followed the trail back towards the snarling and grunting of the grizzly. The beast was in the final frenzy of the slaughter. Storm looked over the scene and nodded to himself after he figured out that his Moon Beam must have somehow strung the man up for the bear. No, Moon Beam wasn't anything like what she appeared to be. She was a slight little woman — but definitely not helpless. In fact, she was quite a deadly killer when provoked.

Storm felt a twinge of sympathy for the stupid man, who was still being mauled by the grizzly. Now Storm was faced with a new challenge. How could he explain to anyone human that Moon Beam was a wolf? And a second thought occurred to him. It was a good thing she liked him a little bit, she might have fed *him* to the grizzly for what he had put her through.

Moon Beam had helped Uncle John back on the horse and was headed back to the cabin with him by the time Storm caught up with them. Once there, she put all her attention into tending to her uncle's needs as he told her about Nels, his greed for money and gold, and his psychotic deeds. Moon Beam just shrugged her shoulders when gold was mentioned, and again when John asked her if there was any more of it lying around. Moon Beam told him that she had never seen gold until it had washed down into a creek bed that ran into the river after the rain. She told him that she had picked up what was lying there, and hadn't noticed any more. Somehow, she seemed to know that the less people knew about the gold, the better off everyone would be.

Storm picked up on this and looked up at Moon Beam as she answered John's question. He knew she was not telling the truth. And he had never heard her

tell a lie. But he knew her well, in spite of their dif-
ferences and their separations. And he knew immediately, by her tone, that Moon Beam knew more than
she was telling.

After recuperating for a few days John felt good
enough to head for home, and he wanted to get there
before a search party was sent out to look for him. He
would have to explain to the town that the man they
had all trusted was not only a thief, but also a ruthless
serial killer. John had no intention of explaining to the
town the gruesome way Nels had met his demise. As
he was leaving, John told Moon Beam that he would
come back in the spring to meet the rest of his family
and to take time to get to know Storm.

Storm had already left for the village to get the
little ones and bring them home to their mother.
Moon Beam was relieved after Storm and John
left. She rested with her wolves and at times lay on
the ground with Shadow holding him close to her.
Shadow loved the extra attention. It had been a long
time since it had been just the two of them. Those
babies he loved so much did cramp his style when it
came to getting attention from Moon Beam but, on
the other hand, he got four times the attention from
the babies. And don't forget, he got in on a lot of
snacks when the human pups were in a sharing mood
— or when they were careless.

CHAPTER 22

The Grizzly's Last Stand

It was late October and a beautiful fall day. The trees were every shade of orange, yellow, and red. Moon Beam hated to have to go in and start supper. As she started to the cabin she thought back to the day Storm had come back with the children after Nels had died. He had brought them home on a couple of paint ponies explaining that it was time they had ponies of their own. Moon Beam nodded her head in agreement with him, and looked down at the floor so he couldn't see the delight in her eyes. He had included their daughters in the gifts.

Storm felt a moment of disappointment when he did not detect any emotion but Moon Beam was reluctant to show her pleasure when he relented and treated the children equally. But as she turned to go Storm's heart leapt in his chest at her words, when she said to the children, "Go thank your father and tell him he's the best father and husband a family could ever have."

That evening, after the children fell asleep Storm and Moon Beam lay on the bear hide in front of the fire entwined in each other's arms. It was the first time in their relationship that she felt there was no tension between them. With neither of them demanding anything from the other they just enjoyed the hours.

With the morning sun, Moon Beam watched Storm ride away, heading back to the village. She felt a twinge of jealousy for the people who had so much of his time. For the first time she wished that she wasn't so low on the list of people he cared for. And, for the first time, she longed to be number one

The children wanted to stay out and play for awhile so Moon Beam called to them to come in closer to the cabin while she went in to make supper. She had just gotten the fire burning nicely and the water on to boil when she heard hair-raising screams from the children.

Having listened to their mother, two of the children were by the cabin entrance, but Brittany Tiny Bird and Ashley Willow were about thirty feet from the cabin. Standing over them was the crazed grizzly. Moon Beam grabbed Sydnee Little Brook and Little Hawk Morgan and pushed them into the cabin. Then, reaching above the door, she grabbed her father's rifle and shoved her knife inside her waistband before reaching for her bow and arrows. She flung the quiver around her neck, never taking her eyes off the bear.

The enormous grizzly rose onto his rear paws and swayed back and forth, throwing his huge head around while roaring and baring his teeth. The two children were frozen to the spot and Moon Beam knew that the minute they made a move to run the bear would attack them.

She raised her rifle to fire just as Storm came through the bush behind the grizzly. Moon Beam was never so happy to see someone in her entire life, but she was surprised, as it was some time ago that he had left for the camp. Never before had he been home when they had really needed him. And they sure did need him now. A cry of alarm and despair escaped from Moon Beam when Storm threw himself on top of the great bear's back. In his hand was the big knife that always hung from his waist. Suddenly, the knife was being plunged to the hilt with every stroke the big man could muster, as he repeatedly sunk the knife into the side of the bear's neck.

At first completely speechless, Moon Beam finally got the danger whistle out of her mouth, calling the pack in. Within a few seconds, the clearing was full of wolves, all attacking the grizzly at the same time. Moon Beam ran towards the children. Wind, who got to them first, stationed his big body in front of them, not moving a muscle. If things went badly and the bear lunged for them, the wolf was prepared to die. Moon Beam finally got to the girls. She pushed Brittany in front of her and scooped Ashley into her arms, making sure not to let go of the rifle, as they ran to the cabin.

Wind backed up to cover them until they reached the safety of the cabin. Only when Moon Beam had the kids safely inside, with the door shut, did the wolf turn and run back to the fight. Moon Beam was right behind him. It was carnage. There were wolves down but the ones still on four paws were fighting for all they were worth. Shadow was giving no ground this time. He remembered. He had waited a long time to settle the score with this killer bear. The bear would die this time. This was the grizzly that had taken his mate, almost killed his mistress, and had nearly finished off the children. Not only that, but on the beast's back was Storm.

The deranged bear had almost killed Storm once before but Shadow had saved him. While hanging on the bear's back, his eyes met Shadow's and he had a flashback. Suddenly, for the first time since that fateful day, Storm remembered the white wolf flying through the air just before he lost consciousness. Funny how things get erased from a person's mind until a similar situation brings them all back. The wolves were keeping the grizzly going around and around in circles, so that Storm could bring the bear down with a final thrust of his knife. Suddenly, in mid-circle, the bear reared straight up, throwing Storm from his perch. The bear whirled around and tried to grab the man from the ground with his claws. Shadow lunged in between them, giving Storm time to regain his feet. Then, gnashing at the bear's hind leg, Shadow got a good grip, his teeth securely holding onto the bear. Pulling with all his might, he somehow pulled the bear over.

As the grizzly fell, Storm realized that the bear was about to come down right over top of him. Storm knew his only chance of survival was to go in tight against the bear's belly. As the grizzly recovered his footing and stood up, so did Storm. He slashed and stabbed at the bear's middle, determined that this time the bear was going to die. Then a shot rang out. The bear fell onto Storm's body. Storm was a tall and muscular man, but the grizzly out-weighed him by hundreds of pounds, covering him completely.

Moon Beam, who had remained calm throughout, had taken careful aim at the bear's head as it began to rise again. But she couldn't shoot until the grizzly was away from Storm and the wolves. Then, when she saw that Storm's head was tucked into the bear's belly, she fired, bringing the grizzly down again. Moon Beam didn't know if Storm was dead or alive. In the last fleeting glimpse she had of him he was pressed up against the bear with the bear trying to claw at him.

By this time Moon Beam was hysterical as she ran towards the bear in a feeble attempt to pull the beast off Storm. Shadow knew that he had to help pull and he yelped for the others to pull with their teeth. They pulled enough for Moon Beam to grab Storm's arm. She screamed at Shadow to grab the man's other arm with his teeth and pull with her. With the other wolves pulling at the bear and Moon Beam and Shadow pulling on the man, out came Storm's big body. He was able to help them with the little strength he had left, and together they pushed away from the bear.

Storm sat up and Moon Beam threw herself into his arms screaming and crying and kissing his face over and over. She couldn't believe he was still alive and kept wetting his face with her tears. Once things calmed down they discovered the worst wound on his body was where Shadow's teeth had sunk into his arm to pull him from the bear. The rest were messy gashes and deep scratches, but he knew he could live with them. They were nothing compared to the last time the bear attacked him. And he knew he couldn't have taken that bear down without the wolves and Moon Beam.

Once the danger had passed, it dawned on Moon Beam that she really did love this man. When she had thought him dead she had felt an unbelievable loss, a flood of sorrow. And all of a sudden she couldn't imagine life without him. She loved him! Moon Beam loved everything about this arrogant man. At long last, she realized and accepted that his arrogance was part of his nature. To her astonishment she realized that she loved him just the way he was. Again she kissed him and this time with genuine tenderness and passion. Storm had no choice but to keep kissing her back. Then he laughed, gave her a big hug, and laboriously picked himself and Moon Beam up off the ground. Then he turned his attention to the big wolf.

Moon Beam held her breath as Storm approached Shadow. And as he reached out to the wolf, love and deep affection filled his heart. Shadow seemed to sense the amazing transformation in the man and went to meet him. The big white wolf stood up on his hind legs and, putting his paws on the man's shoulders, licked his face. Storm laughed and tears came to his eyes as he hugged the big wolf to him. Wind and Salt stood nearby waiting their turns. Their full acceptance of the man had come when they all fought the grizzly together. And all of them, man, woman, and wolves, realized that they each needed the other.

When all the hugging and petting subsided they turned to Moon Beam. Without her they would still be fighting the bear or be dead. Moon Beam, being the Great Wolf, was expected to protect them. That was her job and this situation was really no different than others ... she protected them and they protected her. They all walked towards Moon Beam who was crying again. She was so proud of her wolves, and especially her man. For the first time in seven long years Moon Beam couldn't wait to be in his arms.

Storm's smouldering look indicated that he knew what was on his Moon Beam's mind. And he also knew that his woman had loved him all along. She just hadn't known it. From now on life would be good for his little family.

The sounds of crying little humans brought them back to reality. Moon Beam hurried to the cabin and wiped their tear-stained faces with cool water, comforting them and reassuring them that it was all over. She said, "Come, your father is here." And they followed her back out to Storm and the wolves. Storm stopped digging a hole for the dead wolves as they approached. He watched as Moon Beam and the children walked from wolf to wolf murmuring their goodbyes. A few of the survivors would have to be stitched up, but for now they lay resting. She would fix them up a little later. She checked each one carefully to make sure it wasn't slowly bleeding to death. As Storm resumed his digging, he saw that Moon Beam was trying to hold back her tears for her dead wolves, and he gently said, "Weep for your family and friends Moon Beam. Help them on their way. You are one of them." And Moon Beam wept.

Things were just settling down when suddenly Black, who Moon Beam hadn't seen in a couple of days, galloped into the clearing. He had heard the gunshot and knew she only used that gun when there was real danger. He thundered in, right past Moon Beam, Storm, and the children. From his throat came a primal unearthly scream as he ran at the grizzly. To everyone's alarm and horror the bear was still alive, struggling to regain his footing. Then, in the next instant, the horse's front hooves came down on the monster's head — again and again — until there was not much left of the bear's face. When Black was spent, Storm walked over to the grizzly and slashed its throat.

Moon Beam headed for the cabin. There was supper to prepare, little ones to get ready for bed, and water and wood to be brought in. Then … just maybe … she and her man would lie in front of the fire in each other's arms. She might even tell him about the rest of the gold. Moon Beam smiled and laughed inside … she might even tell him about the secret room. But then again … she might not.

Maybe they would just make love and tell each other how happy they were. That would be better than talking about gold.

LaVergne, TN USA
25 February 2010
174277LV00005B/1/P